SHORT SUBJECT

A Richard Jackson Book

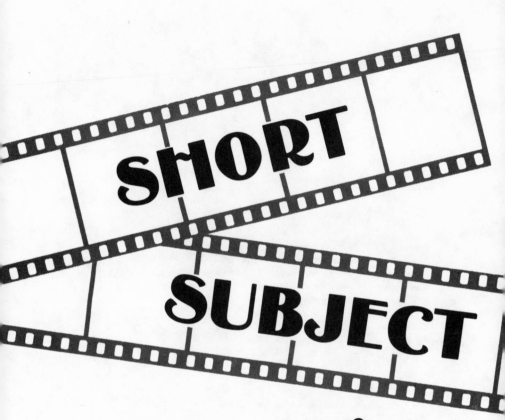

SHORT SUBJECT

Binnie Kirshenbaum

Orchard Books · New York
A division of Franklin Watts, Inc.

Orchard Books, a division of Franklin Watts, Inc.
387 Park Avenue South, New York, NY 10016

Manufactured in the United States of America
Book design by Mina Greenstein
The text of this book is set in 12 pt. Electra
10 9 8 7 6 5 4 3 2 1

Library of Congress Cataloging-in-Publication Data
Kirshenbaum, Binnie.
Short subject / Binnie Kirshenbaum.
p.   cm. "A Richard Jackson book."
Summary: Audrey, who sees her whole life in terms of the old movies
she watches constantly, dreams of finding glory by becoming the kind
of gangster she views in those films.
ISBN 0-531-05836-0.   ISBN 0-531-08436-1 (lib. bdg.)
[1. Self-perception—Fiction.] I. Title. PZ7.K6385Sh 1989
[Fic]—dc19 89-42538 CIP AC

FOR TONY

SHORT SUBJECT

"MOTHER OF MERCY!" I clutched at my heart. "Is this the end of Rico?" Those were Edward G. Robinson's last words in *Little Caesar*, when he played the King of the Underworld. This is the story of how I, Audrey Alice Feldman, almost ended up like him.

"I'm very serious, Audrey," Gertie was saying. Gertie's my mother. She had decided that I watched too many movies. It wasn't healthy, she went on, for me to be spending so much time alone in the dark. "One movie a week. No more." The way she wanted it, that one movie should be on Saturday afternoons. "With your little girlfriends."

I wasn't the only one spending a lot of time in the dark. My little girlfriends. Very funny. The girls in my class are hardly little. On Saturday afternoons, they're caught up with boys. I didn't stand a chance at convincing one of them to come to the movies with me.

1

I wasn't caught up with boys. I was—and still am—too short.

Veronica Lake was very short, yet hardly anyone ever realized that about her. A while ago I tried wearing my hair like she did in the movies, dipped over one eye. Gertie had an attack about that. She claimed I'd go blind. Also, she said that hairstyle didn't look nice. "Not nice" for Gertie equaled "sexy." I had a strong hunch she cared more about my not looking nice than she did about the possibility of my going blind. So she bought me a pair of dinky barrettes, with butterflies on them, no less. Each morning she stood over me making sure I clipped my hair back. "I won't have you losing your vision over some crazy hairstyle," she said.

"Veronica Lake wore her hair like this for years," I said, "and she never lost her eyesight."

"You're not Veronica Lake," Gertie replied.

This was too true. Veronica Lake may have been short but she was also developed. And I was not. I'd been working hard on that, but the facts were that at fourteen plus one month, I could barely pass for ten.

There might have been some eleven-year-old out there who thought I was hot stuff, but the boys in my class brushed by me like I didn't exist. Not that I blamed them. If I were a boy, I wouldn't have given me a second glance either. Not with girls like Lisa Rosenthal and Marcy Tuchman around. With me as the obvious exception, the rule of thumb around Canarsie is early blossoming, rapid maturation. I think there's something in our water. The girls in my class look to be at least seventeen. Those girls are built.

2

Gertie called my father, Herb, into the kitchen for backup. He told me I ought to spend more time with children my own age and I needed fresh air.

I didn't bother pointing out that people my own age are no longer children. However, I did remind him that the air quality in Brooklyn is one step removed from being poison and, on the whole, it was probably safer for my lungs to be in an air-conditioned movie theatre.

"Listen to your mother," was Herb doing his best at being a concerned father. He was never the type to have heart-to-heart chats or to issue sound advice. Herb pretty much ignored the fact that he had three children until one of them (usually me) did something Gertie told him could not be ignored. Then his face would go very red like it was about to pop and he'd sputter and wave his arms. I used to think he might take off and fly around the apartment the way a balloon does when you let out the air.

Like everyone else in my family, Herb had no idea what it is to be a movie fan.

Movies are my life. When I can't be at the Variety I watch late-night television, the next best thing to the big screen. Late-night is better than prime-time because during the family hours they make a lame try for realism, which I find to be dull viewing. Also, it's late at night that TV airs the better movies. By better, I mean old. I've never much cared for the new ones. Too often they're about teenagers. I'm stuck with people my own age all day at school. Who needs to pay good money to see more of them? New movies tend

3

to be about regular people. For my ticket, I'm after glamor.

My sister, Ruth, who is a senior at Hunter College where she majors in psychology, calls movies "escapism." For all her schooling, Ruth doesn't know beans about some areas. The reason for this is she almost never goes to the movies. She is forever telling me how I ought to get out in the world and experience life. I've tried to explain to her that you learn things from movies that experience could never teach you, but Ruth doesn't buy that.

The only connection my brother Alex has to movies is his type shows up in a lot of them. In the movie world, Alex is what's known as a rat, a dirty rat. If they ever make a movie about me, Alex could be played by Victor McLaglen. He's the snitch in *The Informer*, which is practically Alex's life story.

"So," Gertie said, "it's settled then. We'll give you money for one movie a week. One only. Is that clear? Now, you'll need how much?"

Just like that, I was into crime.

"Seven dollars," I told her, which was, in itself, not an out-and-out lie. Seven dollars is the price of an adult ticket at most movie theatres in Brooklyn. "And I need another two dollars for soda and popcorn," I said.

Gertie preferred that I didn't eat such garbage. According to her, soda rots the entire digestive tract from the teeth all the way through the intestines. "Soda eats holes in the stomach," she said. As for popcorn, Gertie simply did not understand popcorn. "What is it any-way?" she used to ask.

"But Gertie," I said, "all the kids have soda and popcorn at the movies. All my little girlfriends." Gertie gave in on the soda and popcorn issue but, as she let me know, this decision was against her better judg-ment. "Only once a week, it couldn't hurt all that much, I guess," she said.

From then on, every Saturday morning Gertie would wipe her hands on her apron and count out nine singles for me. Before forking the money over, she insisted upon telling me—each time—"When I was a girl the movies cost fifty cents. And with that same fifty cents you got free jujubes and a set of dishes."

The scam was that the Variety Theatre, which was the only movie house I went to, charged $2.50 for an adult ticket and seventy-five cents for the under-twelve crowd. Even though I had not been under twelve for a couple of years, Mr. Eisenstein, who owned and managed the Variety, let me in for kid's price anyway. Plus, he gave me a cut rate of fifty cents on the popcorn, with butter even, because I was his best customer. For this same reason, Mr. Eisenstein treated me to my sodas, and so Gertie's nine bucks went for a movie every day of the week. That left me with a quarter. There's nothing you can do with a quarter, so each week I put it in the tin can Mr. Eisenstein kept on the candy counter. It went to charity. A lot of crooks have hearts of gold and think nothing of giving some of their loot to the less fortunate.

My modus operandi was unvarying. That means I did the same thing every day. After school let out, I'd head straight for the Variety and sit in the lobby yakking with Mr. Eisenstein until the four o'clock show. Mr. Eisenstein never showed the same movie two days in a row because his audience wasn't big enough for that. Also, he maintained that with so many great movies out there, even at one a day, it would take over thirty years to show them all.

Every day at five minutes to four, I'd find my seat and get comfortable in it. Mine was the bull's-eye seat, dead center, the middle seat in the middle row. Even though Mr. Eisenstein claimed he did a halfway decent business in the evenings—"People always want to see the classics," he'd say—the theatre was always nearly deserted in the afternoons. There was never more than a handful of us hardcore movie fans there for the four o'clock showing. I liked it better that way, preferring not to sit too close to anyone else. A person sitting right next to you in the movies can interfere with your escape onto the screen.

There is something magical about those few moments in the theatre when it's dark and you're waiting for the curtain to open. It's like you're taking a secret trip, so secret not even you know where you're going.

This four o'clock showing let us out before six which put me in Gertie's kitchen no later than six-fifteen, a half hour before dinner, and no one was ever the wiser.

It was a snap to lie to Gertie about where I'd been all afternoon. Sometimes I'd say I stayed after school to use the library. That was a personal favorite of

6

Herb's. Other times I would say I went to the park, which never failed to make my mother nervous until I'd add, "With my little girlfriends."

"Oh," Gertie said then, "okay. I don't want you going to the park alone. It's dangerous in the park with all the crazy people on the loose."

The best lie I came up with was the one where I said I'd joined the choir at school. Choir practice accounted for months of afternoons. I would have stayed with that one for longer had Gertie not kept after me to sing her a little something. So I switched and said things like, "I was at a friend's house."

"You know," Gertie would say then, "you could bring your friends here sometimes. You're ashamed of us or something that you don't bring your friends here?"

The truth of the matter was that Mr. Eisenstein was the only friend I had. And he wasn't exactly my friend, because I couldn't call him on the phone or go to the mall with him or anything like that. But I did like to yak with him before the movies started. He was A-OK for an old person. As a rule, old people tended to pat me on the head and talk to me like I was around two years old. Sometimes, like Mrs. Shilling in our building, they went so far as to make goo-goo sounds at me. Not Mr. Eisenstein though. He knew a real movie fan when he saw one and he had respect for that no matter what the person's size. He talked to me like we were the same age. Mr. Eisenstein knew more about the movies than Cecil B. De Mille, Sam Goldwyn, and Rex Reed combined.

Mr. Eisenstein offered good movie advice. Movies

he highly recommended were so great that I'd wonder how I'd managed to live so long without seeing them before. Equally, he steered me clear of clunkers. There weren't many of those because like I always say, every movie has its redeeming moments. But there were a few without any. Take *San Francisco*. "Don't bother coming tomorrow," Mr. Eisenstein had said. *"San Francisco."* He pinched his nose like there was a bad smell around. "Stinks," he said. "Jeanette MacDonald at her worst. Pee-ew. Save your money, Audrey."

San Francisco was the one movie which Gertie had raved about. That should have been a tip-off by itself. What interested me in seeing *San Francisco* was the earthquake part. "Doesn't it have that great earthquake scene?" I asked Mr. Eisenstein. Ever since seeing *The Last Days of Pompeii*, I was dying to catch another disaster scene. No one made disaster like Hollywood.

"Take my word for it, Audrey," Mr. Eisenstein said, "The earthquake is a good moment but not worth waiting for. I show this movie for the old ladies. They love it. But it's not for you."

When I showed up the next day anyway, Mr. Eisenstein wagged a finger at me and said, "I warned you."

By the time San Francisco exploded into flames, I was glad to see it go. Mr. Eisenstein knew his stuff all right.

One time, looking out only for his interests and surely not my own, I asked Mr. Eisenstein if he wouldn't make more money by showing new movies at the Variety. I couldn't help but notice that other movie theatres had people standing on line for tickets. I worried about the Variety's thin crowd and wondered how much rent money they brought in.

Mr. Eisenstein shrugged and said, "Maybe. Who cares? Tell me, Audrey, did you ever hear of a director named Eisenstein?"

I'd never heard of the guy. "No," I said. "Is he a cousin of yours?"

"Nah. He was a very famous director years ago. Maybe the greatest. A Russian. You heard of *The Battleship Potemkin*? What about *Ivan the Terrible* Parts One and Two? Or *Ten Days That Shook the World*? You ever hear of any of those movies?"

I shook my head.

"The man was a genius," Mr. Eisenstein told me. "Someday, you'll have the good fortune to see Sergei Eisenstein's movies and you'll know for yourself. Fantastic movies. Innovative. Brilliant. In the meantime, that Eisenstein's mission was to make great movies and this Eisenstein's mission is to show great movies. I owe it to him, no? With a name like Eisenstein, you want me to show *Porky's*? Now, go. The movie's about to begin."

4 3 2 1

I DIDN'T always go to the movies alone. I used to go with Rosalie.

Rosalie was also a movie fan, which I considered my good luck. After all, what were the odds of there being two movie fans our age in Canarsie? The only hitch was that Rosalie's taste in movies often ran in the direction of sap. For example, Rosalie was mad for *National Velvet*. I had to sit through *National Velvet* twice at the movies and once on television because that was our understanding. Rosalie and I had an agreement. I had to suffer through the dopey movies she liked and she had to sit with me for my picks. It was rough for me to get worked up over a young Elizabeth Taylor on a horse. I liked my heroines to be the sort who didn't mind parading around in a tattered slip and dating gangsters. Rosalie favored the ones who wore hats and gloves and triumphed. My heroines usually

10

ended up in the gutter at the end of the movie. Rosalie even liked Doris Day.

Rosalie's very favorite movies were the ones where the lowly chorus girl makes it to the top because she's so sweet and is able to tap dance up a storm. I suspected Rosalie had similar plans for herself, because on Tuesdays she took tap-dance lessons with Mr. Frederick. He had a fake French accent and a Clark Gable mustache, which looked a whole lot better on Clark Gable. In a number of ways, Rosalie was a piece of fluff. Still, she was my best friend.

We were coming home from seeing *Cover Girl* when Rosalie gave me the news. That was a year ago. *Cover Girl* starred Gene Kelly and Rita Hayworth. I had assumed we'd sit through it twice because it was a Saturday and we always sat through the movie twice on Saturdays. But this time Rosalie didn't want to. This took me by surprise. *Cover Girl* was strictly her kind of movie.

Rosalie said she had to talk to me. So we left and were halfway to her house when she gave me the scoop. Her family was moving to Long Island and taking Rosalie with them.

No one ever expected them to stay in the Canarsie section of Brooklyn forever. Canarsie never fit them quite right. "Fancy-schmancy," Gertie used to call Rosalie's family. "Such precious furniture no one can sit on it. And you have to take off your shoes in their home," Gertie would go on. "The mother invites me over for a cup of tea and tells me I have to take off my shoes. What's the matter? My dirt isn't good enough for her?"

Although she never put it this way, Gertie thought Rosalie's mother unfit. "The woman is never home," Gertie said very often. "And when she is home she parades around like a teenager." Rosalie's mother wore blue jeans and had a part-time job as a receptionist in an office building. My opinion, although no one ever asked for it, was that Gertie was a little jealous of Rosalie's mother. Like a lot of the Canarsie mothers, Gertie sampled her own cooking too much. "How do I know if it needs more salt unless I taste it first?" was her excuse for being sort of fat.

Rosalie's mother did not cook. Mostly Rosalie had pizza or sandwiches to eat. The pantry at their house contained the biggest collection of chips and pretzels and cakes and nuts I'd seen outside of the A&P. Rosalie's kitchen was stuffed with the sort of food Gertie wouldn't have allowed past our threshold; food like peanut-butter cups and marshmallows and packaged white bread. Gertie believed that packaged white bread was a killer. "It's like eating air," she said. "Bad air."

To me, white bread was angel's food and I liked almost nothing more than to sit with Rosalie in her kitchen, without some mother breathing down our necks, and roll the bread into dough balls, the way you could never do with rye or pumpernickel, and pop them into our mouths.

Everything was always more fun at Rosalie's. Whenever she came to my house, Gertie would grab her by the upper arm and say, "You're too skinny, Rosalie.

12

You look like you've been living on packaged white bread. What's the matter, your mother never feeds you?" And then Gertie would force feed us baked chicken. At Rosalie's house, we got some privacy.

We did always expect them to move. We always thought Rosalie's family would move to a more elegant part of Brooklyn like Mill Basin or Park Slope. But I never considered Long Island. You can't even get to Long Island on the subway.

Rosalie and I went into her kitchen to eat Cheez Whiz on crackers and discuss this move. We sat at her kitchen table, first squirting the bacon-flavored cheddar on our fingers which we used as a knife. "So," I said, "Long Island, huh?"

"Please, Audrey." Rosalie squirted a string of cheese directly into her mouth. She looked like a baby bird with a worm, something I'd only seen on educational television which Herb used to make me watch. "I'm sick about it," Rosalie said. "Just sick."

It was sweet of her to say she was unhappy about the move, even though I doubted her sincerity. Not that I blamed her any. I don't think I would have exactly broken down and wept if my family were to move to Bellmore, Long Island. And take me with them.

Bellmore, Long Island, sounded like yachts and Alan Ladd. I'd seen *The Great Gatsby*, so I knew a good deal about Long Island and places with names like Bellmore. That was part of the beauty of movies. You could visit foreign and exotic lands without ever leaving your seat. I knew Rosalie was destined to loll around on white wicker lawn chairs and sip lemonade. I knew that, in no time flat, she'd be playing golf instead of stoopball.

Rosalie told me her parents had bribed her with a new bedroom set if she wouldn't throw a tantrum about moving away. "You should see it, Audrey," she said. "I picked it out from a magazine. It's going to be a living module with hi-tech track lighting." I pictured this to be right out of science fiction. Rosalie told me a living module was the latest in bedroom designs. "It's way cool," she said, and I wondered where Rosalie had picked up such an expression. Not from the movies, that's for sure.

I wondered what was wrong with the bedroom set Rosalie already had. I thought it was swell. Rosalie's bedroom in Canarsie was all white. Her desk and dresser and shelving even matched; they all had little lavender flowers gracing the edges. It looked to me like a set for a movie. It was that pretty. Plus, it suited Rosalie's personality. But Rosalie said she was tired of it. "I'm ready for a change," she said.

I'd never seen a living module except maybe in a movie called *The Space Children*. The space children lived in a room which was all angles and corners and geometric planes until another creature came and made a mess of the place. This creature was made from Jell-O and he oozed everywhere.

Rosalie vowed I would see her living module. "All the time," she said, slinging her arm around my shoulder. "As soon as it's finished you can come out for the weekend. Every weekend, if you want."

14

AS ROSALIE'S departure date for Bellmore, Long Island, grew closer and closer, it came to me that we should make a pact. An eternal vow to be friends forever. In the movies, the good Indian brave and the one white man who isn't a total slug always become blood brothers. Buddies for life. I wanted Rosalie and me to do something like that. Knowing I'd never get Rosalie to draw blood, I hit upon the idea of exchanging locks of hair. "We can put it in boxes," I told her, "and sleep with it under our pillows."

"Our hair?" Rosalie's hand shot protectively to her curls. Rosalie's curls meant as much to her as they would to a young Shirley Temple. Rosalie's curls were springy and blond and the pride of her life. She wasn't too keen about parting with one.

"One small curl from underneath," I said. "You won't even know it's gone. I promise."

From Gertie's sewing basket I took the scissors, and

15

I got two envelopes from Herb's desk. I led Rosalie out of my apartment and into the alleyway. Alleyways were used for storing trash until the garbage men came for it on Mondays and Thursdays.

"It smells out here." Rosalie pinched her nose. Rosalie's tendency to be the delicate flower sometimes got on my nerves.

"Do you want to make an eternal vow of friendship or not?" I asked.

Rosalie shrugged. "You go first."

It was no big deal to go first. In the movies, the Indian always went first. I lifted a lock of hair from the top of my head, held it straight up, and snipped. I put my hair in one of the envelopes and sealed it shut.

Rosalie hesitated before taking it from me. "It's kind of creepy," she said.

Holding the scissors out for her, I said, "It's your turn," but Rosalie kept her arms pinned to her sides. "You do it for me," she said. Rosalie couldn't bear taking her own curl.

"Okay." I sifted through her hair to get some from underneath. As if this were going to hurt, Rosalie clamped her eyes shut and trembled. "Quit shaking," I said. "It's only hair."

"That's easy for you to say. You don't have blond curls." Rosalie could be kind of snotty when she wanted to.

I got hold of a tiny lock from behind her ear. I instructed her to stay still, quit squirming, for one second. Just as I cut, Rosalie pulled back and twisted away. Some extra hair got tangled in the scissor, so instead of one small curl, I clipped off a pretty good-sized chunk.

Rosalie took one look at her curls on the ground and the blond hairs still tangled in the scissors, and she gave out a shriek. Snatching up the fallen curls, she put the hair to her head as if she could stick it back on. "Oh, my hair. My beautiful golden hair." Rosalie was sort of hysterical.

I tried talking some sense into her. "You pulled away," I reasoned. "You weren't supposed to pull away. It's only hair, Rosalie."

Rosalie refused to listen to reason, and she ran home clutching her curls in her fist.

Later that night, Gertie got a phone call. When she hung up, she marched into the living room and snapped off the TV. Her arms crossed over her bosom. This was a sure sign I was in some kind of trouble.

"That was Rosalie's mother on the telephone. They had to take her to an expensive hairdresser to cover up what you did. Whatever possessed you to hack away at her hair? With scissors, no less. You could've poked out her eye with those scissors. What's the matter with you?"

From his post in the kitchen where he was doing homework, Alex answered for me. "She's crazy," he shouted. "Deranged."

"It was an accident," I explained.

"You were playing with scissors," Gertie said. "That

was no accident. The scissors did not jump out of my sewing basket and into your hands." Gertie wanted to know where were the brains God gave me.

"God didn't give her any brains," Alex piped in. "A person with brains doesn't spend all their waking hours staring at a screen."

Gertie didn't tell Alex to quit picking at me. Around our house, Alex is considered the Crown Prince of Brooklyn. Instead, I was given strict orders. I was never, ever, under any circumstances to take scissors to another person's hair again. "For that matter," Gertie went on, "don't touch scissors again for any reason. Or knives. Or anything sharp. If you need to cut something, you come to me first."

Rather than going back to the TV, I decided to give Rosalie a call. She answered on the second ring, which was a relief. I'd had a bellyful of parents by that point. I wasn't too interested in having to talk to hers.

"Hi," I said. "It's me. Audrey."

"Oh. Hello." Rosalie was distinctly cool.

"Listen, I really am sorry about your hair. I heard you got it fixed. Does it look okay?"

"Yes. You can't tell that you wrecked it unless you look closely. Mother took me to Jean Pierre. He's a genius and very expensive." Rosalie was warming up. I knew she wouldn't stay mad at me for long. Rosalie was a marshmallow. Plus, she was thrilled to get to go to Jean Pierre. "Everything at Jean Pierre's is French," she told me. "He barely speaks English. We were very lucky to get an appointment."

18

"Yeah. Well, that's good." I didn't want to talk about hair anymore. I couldn't figure what all the fuss was about. After all, it grows back. "Listen, I've got a surprise for you." This surprise was one I'd known about for a few days but figured this was a good time to spring on her. "Guess what's playing at the Variety on Saturday." On Sunday, Rosalie was moving away for good. "*42nd Street*," I told her, because Rosalie couldn't guess.

We'd seen *42nd Street* before. Personally, I thought it was a dud but Rosalie was wild about it. It might've been her favorite movie ever. She'd gone so far as to learn all the songs and she could do a fair impression of Ruby Keeler tap dancing.

"Oh, I hope I can go," Rosalie said. "I might have to stay around because of the move. We still have some last minute packing to do. I'll have to get back to you, okay?"

IT TURNED out Rosalie didn't get back to me, so I went to see *42nd Street* by myself. I haven't a clue why I went to such a dorky picture when I didn't have to, except any movie was better than doing nothing.

When the movie was over, I took the long way home. Ever since I'd cut Rosalie's hair, my family had been treating me like a knife-wielding maniac. Gertie was going so far as to cut up my meat for me. Before leaving the apartment I was practically frisked by Herb. And Ruth had sat me down to tell me such accidents were really repressed anger. She actually said I was acting out hostility because I was mad at Rosalie for moving away. That was so ridiculous. Rosalie wouldn't have moved if she had any say in the matter. Anyway, was it any wonder I took a few detours on the way home?

When I did get there, the superintendent's dog was sitting on the steps to our building. As I approached, he thumped his tail at me. This dog was no Rin Tin Tin. Or even a Lassie. He was just a mangy mutt, a small dog with lots of hair the color of a mouse. But while he would never win any blue ribbons at a dog show, he was a very nice mutt. I played with him sometimes.

I sat down on the steps next to him. He moved in closer until he was practically in my lap. I patted him on the head and scratched him behind the ears. He was mad for the scratching behind the ears.

It was only because I was in the mood to gab that I filled the dog in on the plot of *42nd Street*. If a person were around, I would've told them instead. But there wasn't a person around and talking to a dog is not as pathetic as talking to yourself. Plus, the mutt seemed very interested. He looked up at me with his big pooch eyes, so I figured, "Why not?" and I sang him one of the songs. When I finished, he licked my hand and, honest, that almost made me cry. The miserable little dog didn't have a friend in the world.

I stayed with him until dinner time when I knew that if I weren't at the table Gertie would send a squadron of coppers out looking for me. Patting the dog once more, I walked up the three flights to our apartment.

The hallway stunk because Mrs. Berman was cooking cabbage again.

The exact second I let myself in, Gertie shouted at me to wash my hands. "I saw you touching that dirty dog," she said. "Dogs are covered with germs and bacteria. Now, quick. Wash your hands with hot water before you get sick."

Although I did go directly to the bathroom and turn on the hot water, I didn't wash my hands. I just stood around and watched the steam fog up the mirror long enough for Gertie to believe I was dog-germ free.

In THE Canarsie section of Brooklyn, a moving van parked on the block was an event. The moving van that came to cart away Rosalie's family and their junk was no exception. I was out with the rest of the neighborhood watching the men, directed by Rosalie's father, load up the Mayflower truck. What puzzled me was why they hired such a big moving van when they were taking almost nothing with them. It was like they were leaving the past behind, starting fresh. They weren't about to have all that old stuff around as a reminder. The little they did take could've easily been hauled off in a Checker cab. I'd heard Mrs. Berman say Rosalie's mother had donated most of their furniture to Goodwill. Mrs. Berman said this as if she were peeved that Rosalie's mother hadn't given her the dinette set.

I figured Rosalie hadn't yet said good-bye because she couldn't find me in the crowd. I figured I'd better try to find her. Standing on my tiptoes was useless so

I climbed up on the roof of a parked car. It was the only way I could see over all the people. Sure enough, from that lookout I spotted Rosalie standing by the left side of the moving van. Her hair looked exactly the same.

I jumped down from the car and made my way over to her. I pushed past a group of ladies who were making snide comments about Rosalie's mother's silver couch. "Rosalie! Hey, Rosalie! Over here!" I called.

We met up by the van's tires. "Oh Audrey, I'm so glad you found me. I was looking all over for you. And don't worry, I'm not mad at you anymore."

"Mad at me for what?" I asked.

"My hair. Jean Pierre works wonders, don't you agree?" She turned in a little circle so I could see from all sides.

"Yeah. It looks great. Better than before."

"Yes, it does." Rosalie could really get hung up on herself but this wasn't the time to be listing her faults.

"So, give me a call when you get settled in," I said, "and I'll come for the weekend."

"Oh, yes. I promise. You can come all the time. And I'll come back to Brooklyn and visit you." Rosalie wiped away a tear.

"Rosalie!" her mother called. "Let's go."

Rosalie turned to her mother and then back to me. She gave me a big hug and said, "I'll never be able to see a movie without thinking of you. I'm going to miss you bunches."

"Don't go and get so gushy, Rosalie. I'll see you in a couple of weeks."

But gushy was Rosalie's style. She squeezed my hand and her eyes got all dewy like she was going to start blubbering.

"Rosalie!" her mother called again and Rosalie gave me one more hug before running off.

The moving men shut the doors to the truck and climbed into the cab. They honked the horn and the mob scene on the street parted like the Red Sea in Bible movies. The van drove away followed by Rosalie, her parents, and her dopey little brother in their sky-blue LeMans. As they passed, I waved to Rosalie and Rosalie waved back until their car was out of sight.

FOR A while after Rosalie moved away, I used to imagine the craziest thing. I kept picturing her in a Busby Berkeley musical. I saw Rosalie in a pink evening gown and patent leather tap-dance shoes standing at the top of a white marble circular staircase. At the foot of the staircase was what appeared to be a rose garden. The centerpiece was Carmen Miranda with a basket of fruit for a hat. As Rosalie tapped her way down the stairs, the garden bloomed. Only the flowers weren't really flowers. They were other dancers. The chorus line doing a ballet. When Rosalie reached the bottom, she grabbed her school books off a shelf. This upset the fruitbowl on Carmen Miranda's head. But Rosalie didn't even apologize because that was the sort of person Rosalie turned out to be. While Carmen Miranda scooped her grapes and pineapples off the floor, Rosalie flurried out the door on her way to school.

This was, of course, pure kookball fantasy on my

part. I quit imagining it after a while. By then I'd figured out what really happened to Rosalie was she'd made a pile of new friends. She was probably dating boys with names like Bud or Charles, boys who drove sports cars and would never have been friends with James Dean. It was also very likely that Rosalie grew breasts the same weekend she moved to Long Island. And no doubt she highlighted them by wearing cashmere sweaters. Rosalie must've forgotten all about Brooklyn in no time flat. That was okay by me. I more or less forgot all about Rosalie, too.

I'D STOPPED growing in any direction when I was nine and a half, which left me at four foot eight with the same build as Alfalfa in *The Little Rascals*.

Gertie was fond of telling me that every cloud has shiny insides, meaning I should be an optimist. For a role model, Gertie took me to see the movie *Pollyanna*. This was the only movie Gertie ever took me to. It was so sugary-sweet, it made me sick. Hayley Mills, as Pollyanna, was a living, breathing ray of sunshine who turned my stomach over. "See," Gertie said after the movie, "she found the shiny parts in the clouds."

Gertie actually expected me to buy this sort of bunky philosophy for myself. "Believe me," Gertie said, "there are many advantages to being small. When you're thirty, you'll be grateful for your baby face."

The problem the way I saw it was not my baby face but my baby body. "When will I be grateful for that?" I asked. Gertie did not have any more answers.

There were, in fact, a couple of bonuses to being my size, things Gertie didn't know about. Aside from getting in for kid's prices at the movies and the roller rink, my size allowed me to become a master at gathering information. I was good for more gossip in my neighborhood than anyone. Except maybe Mrs. Korngold. She made it her life's business to find out the inside scoop.

As grown-ups tended to forget, or not realize in the first place, how old I actually was, they talked freely in front of me. All I had to do was sit there quietly and they'd spill the beans directly into my ears.

Even my own parents did this. And they knew for a fact how old I was. Plus, they also knew that my reading comprehension was on a college level. I'm not bragging. I'd been tested and had it authorized on paper. Besides, the movies I went to weren't exactly Disney material. Therefore, when my mother told Mrs. Shilling that Mrs. Horowitz was running around with the dentist, I knew perfectly well no one was jogging. Only they didn't know I knew that.

Still, despite these few rewards, the point spread on my condition was uneven. The disadvantages to being a squirt had the yardage by far. For openers, no matter which way you turned me, I was a freak. That is never the sort of thing you pick out for yourself to be.

In Canarsie, if boys don't like you, then no one does. The number of boys chasing after you was the measuring stick of popularity. If you had ten boyfriends, you got voted president of all the clubs and were head cheerleader, too. One boyfriend bought you a cluster of girlfriends and membership to the Pep squad. I measured zero.

For a time, the worst of this was gym class. My undershirt was good for a lot of laughs. Very funny stuff, according to some people. Beverly Shelby called it an antique. She had her gang circle me in the locker room. "Girls," she said, pointing at me like I was an exhibit in a museum, "will you get a load of this? It's an undershirt, isn't it? I ask you, girls, when was the last time you saw one of these?"

And Marie Costello said, "Last night. On my boyfriend."

Elise Winters used to ask if she could touch it for old time's sake.

The way I figured it, if I couldn't have the bosoms, I could at least have the trappings. So at the start of the eighth grade I sat Gertie down and got right to the point. I wanted a bra. Gertie laughed. Gertie is not always a sensitive person. "For what? You have nothing to put in it." My mother thought that was hilarious. She howled and guffawed and for a minute, a very panicked minute, I thought she was going to call Herb in to share this joke.

It was obvious Gertie needed to be filled in about training bras. They must not have had them in her day. "It's nothing more than an elastic band with adjustable straps," I told her. "One size fits all. And they come in pink and baby blue and white and cost three dollars. Mostly, they're for show."

"Show? Who do you have to show? Who's looking?" Gertie wanted to know.

I was not about to tell my mother about my being the hoot of the locker room. Mothers deal with that sort of thing all wrong. They always want to report it to the school principal. Or worse yet, call the other girls' mothers. Mothers can make you look like a snitch when you're not. "Me," I said. "I have me to show. Besides, don't you think maybe a training bra is the incentive I need? I might respond to it. Live up to its expectations."

"An undershirt keeps you warm," Gertie said. "You didn't get one cold last winter, did you?"

The girls at school eventually tired of the same dumb remarks every Tuesday and Thursday morning. They came to leave me alone about my undershirt. Of course, they left me alone about everything else, too. There were actually moments when I thought I liked it better when they made fun of me. At least then they knew I was there.

Since I couldn't have a bra, I tried other props. Things I thought would make me look older. Like makeup. But even I was forced to admit that it had the opposite effect. I looked like some real little kid who was messing around in her mother's cosmetics.

I searched for signs of growth daily. I checked my height against a marking on my wall. Each morning, I got out the tape measure and took my vital statistics. Nothing changed.

One time, Gertie told me I was under-sized because I wasn't eating enough green, leafy vegetables. She said

28

those vegetables contained growth vitamins. Out of sheer desperation, I fell for it. In several weeks, I consumed more spinach than Popeye did in his entire career. All for nothing.

I gave Gertie a good talking to. "How could you lie to me like that?" I asked. "You gave me false hopes just to get me to eat more vegetables. It was a rotten trick," I said. Then I felt even more lousy because she started to cry and hug me. "Be patient," she said. "You'll see. Just be patient."

The problem was I really couldn't be patient much longer. Time was running out. It was one thing to be my size in grade school. There at least I blended in with the fifth graders. But I was about to start ninth grade, and I just couldn't go to high school looking like a Munchkin.

It was my sister Ruth who got them to take me to a specialist doctor. But it wasn't directly her doing because Ruth was too confused a person to have come up with such a seemingly good idea. Ruth wanted Gertie to take me to a psychiatrist. Ruth devised this cockeyed theory about my subconscious having taken control over my body and directing it to stay little.

Even for Gertie, this was too wacky. "Nonsense," she said.

"But, Mother," Ruth said, "something is obviously wrong. It's not normal for her to be that size. You must realize that."

After a cliffhanger of a pause, I heard Gertie say, "You're right. I ought to take her to see someone."

"I know a terrific child psychologist," Ruth said.

"No," Gertie said. "No head doctors. I'll take her to a doctor doctor. A real doctor. Maybe she's missing a gene or something he can give her."

I was so tickled with this idea that I nearly gave myself away by jumping from my hiding spot.

Gertie made an appointment with a Dr. Straub. She told me it was just for a routine checkup but I knew he was the specialist.

During the week before my doctor's appointment, I busied myself making a list of what I wanted. I had to be sure I didn't leave anything out. When I'd finished it, I sat on the steps of our building and ran it by the super's dog. I just wanted to hear how it sounded out loud.

1. Grow nine inches. This would make me 5'5" which is the best height for a girl in high school. Maybe later, add another inch or two in case I decided to be a professional model or a basketball player.
2. Bosoms like Jane Russell's. Not puny ones like my sister Ruth has.
3. Long legs like Betty Grable's.
4. A husky voice like Lauren Bacall's.
5. A waistline.

My guess was that this doctor would give me some pills which would work wonders. Or it was possible that this growth formula came in needles. I once saw a movie where a man got bit by a skunk and had to

30

get rabies shots. It was horrible looking. Still, if that was the only way to grow, I'd take them.

"It's only a matter of weeks," I said to the dog, "before I'll be wearing satin dresses with slits down to here." I pointed at my stomach. "I'll be wearing dresses like Virginia Mayo wore in *White Heat*. I'm going to have cleavage."

7 6 5 4

Dr. Straub's waiting room didn't look special.
It looked almost exactly like Dr. Vaccaro's waiting
room; same sort of ratty couch, magazine rack, and
imitation paintings on the walls. Dr. Vaccaro was our
regular family doctor.

Gertie knitted while I thumbed through a copy of
Reader's Digest. I was too anxious to concentrate much
on what I was reading. Periodically, Gertie leaned over
and told me to sit still. Sitting still held some special
meaning for her.

When the nurse called my name, Gertie got up with
me. Together we went to the nurse's desk. I wasn't too
keen on the idea of Gertie's shadowing me, but my
mother has never been an easy person to ditch. In many
respects, Gertie would have made a good G-man.

The nurse, after checking which one of us was
Audrey Feldman and which of us was Audrey Feldman's mother, handed me a Dixie cup. She told me

32

to fill it up. Gertie was all set to trail me into the bathroom.

"I can manage myself," I told her.

"I know that," Gertie said. Nevertheless, she was on stakeout right outside the bathroom door. She yelled in at me to run the faucet if I was having trouble going.

As it turned out, I missed the cup by a long shot. Not more than a spit's worth hit the target.

"That's all?" Gertie asked, peering into the cup as I came out of the bathroom. "Didn't you drink your juice this morning?"

I didn't answer Gertie but mumbled "Sorry" to the nurse as I handed her the cup. She gave me a purse-lipped nod and I noticed she wasn't all that impressive in the body department either. For the first time, it crossed my mind that this Dr. Straub might not be all I'd cracked him up to be.

After doing a vanishing act with my Dixie cup, the nurse returned and ushered me into the examining room. Gertie came with us.

"Down to your underwear," the nurse told me. I didn't think she'd ever seen the movie *Nurse Edith Cavell*. If she had, her manner would have been different. She would have had compassion. *Nurse Edith Cavell* is a very inspirational movie about a nurse who serves in a war. That movie got me in the heart. After seeing it, I actually considered being a nurse. I considered being a nurse for two days. Then I saw *Skirts Ahoy!* with Esther Williams and Vivian Blaine. That movie made me want to be a girl sailor. Eventually, I realized that as long as I continued going to the movies, I didn't have to be anything. I could be everything for a couple of hours instead.

I stripped down to my sleeveless tee-shirt and white cotton Carters. My stomach stuck out like you see on little girls in their two-piece bathing suits at Coney Island.

The nurse weighed me in at seventy-six pounds. She took my height and raised an eyebrow when she asked my age. She turned to Gertie to see if I was telling the truth about that.

She told me to sit on the table and wait for the doctor. "He'll be right with you," she said before closing the door behind her.

He wasn't right with us at all. Dr. Straub took his sweet time in getting to me. Gertie kept making excuses for him: "A specialist is a very busy man." Meanwhile, I sat on that table feeling as exposed as a plucked chicken.

I was about to get dressed, thinking I'd been forgotten, when Dr. Straub made his big entrance. He looked like Chico Marx only he didn't seem like he'd be as funny. "How are we today, little lady?" he asked, looking down at his charts instead of at me.

"We're fine," Gertie told him.

I said, "The name is Audrey."

"Yes," he said.

Dr. Straub looked into my eyes with a pen-light flashlight. He made a note on my chart so I asked if I were going blind. He didn't answer me. He looked in my ears. He tested my reflexes with a rubber hammer. That is a halfway decent trick if you've never seen it done before. He held my wrist and clocked my pulse. As interesting as all this might have been, I was getting the feeling we were off the track. Then he had me touch my nose with my index finger and I started suspecting the guy was a quack. I suspected he was up against something he knew nothing about. He seemed to be stalling for time.

"Excuse me," I said loudly to get him to look up from his charts, "I want ones like this." I cupped my hands six inches from my chest.

"Open wide and say 'Ahhh.' " He put a Popsicle stick down my throat, scribbled some more on his chart and said to Gertie, "She can get dressed now."

Dr. Straub had Gertie and me meet him in his office. This office was down the hall from the examining room and looked like a study. His diplomas hung on the wall. Gertie was very impressed with all those diplomas. I studied them closely to make sure they weren't fakes.

Gertie and I sat across the desk from Dr. Straub. His desk was cluttered. He fiddled with a pen and pretended to be thinking.

"So," I said, anxious to get the ball rolling, "when do I grow?"

Dr. Straub took a deep breath and said, "Well, young lady . . ."

"Audrey," I said. Gertie shot me a look which read, "Be polite."

"Yes. Audrey. Audrey. Audrey. Well, Audrey. I really don't know." Dr. Straub twisted in his chair so that he faced only Gertie. I was out of his picture.

"The truth is," he said to my mother, "I don't think we ought to do anything just yet. It's not uncommon for girls to have a delayed maturation. And otherwise, your daughter is in perfect health. I think it would be wise of us to sit back for a while longer. Let's give nature a chance."

Gertie was lapping this up. Her head was bobbing like those plastic dolls that perch on dashboards.

"Chances are good," the quack went on, "that she'll develop on her own. Until then, let's be patient. How does that sound?"

I told him it sounded very lousy. But no one seemed to hear me. Dr. Straub continued to talk to Gertie. He told her to see to it I got my rest and ate well-balanced meals. "See to it," he said, "that she gets plenty of exercise. Skipping rope and all that."

Somewhere around the eating well part, I clipped his pen. The one he'd been fiddling with. He put it down and I took it. It wasn't a fancy pen. No sterling silver Cross pen or anything like that. It was just your standard twenty-five-cent plastic pen, but I had the feeling he was rather attached to it. Pretending to adjust my waistband, I stuck it down my underpants.

He let us know he was done with us by standing up and saying, "See the nurse on the way out." This was not because she wanted to say good-bye or good luck. He just wanted to be sure we didn't skip out without paying him. I could've been Dorothy when Toto pulled back the curtain and exposed the Wizard of Oz as a nobody.

While Gertie and I waited for the number seven bus, I told her I thought we ought to get a second opinion. To Gertie, getting a second opinion on a doctor meant asking God. She rated doctors that high up. "I thought he was an excellent doctor," she said. "A lovely man. And so many diplomas. So impressive. He looked a little familiar to me. Did he look a little familiar to you?"

"Yeah," I said. "He looked like a Marx brother. Chico. He looked like Chico Marx playing one of Dr. Hackenbush's assistants."

"Don't be fresh," Gertie said.

We boarded the bus. I had to sit leaning toward the left because the pen was digging into me. Gertie took this to mean I wanted to stare out the window. That was fine by me. I pretended to be absorbed with the traffic on the street and Gertie struck up a conversation with a woman across the aisle.

THE SUPER'S dog was waiting for me on the steps. "They ought to keep that animal tied up some-place," Gertie said.

I looked at the little mutt and then back to Gertie. "Yeah," I said. "He looks real fierce."

Gertie told me not to be so disrespectful. Still, she cut short the rest of the lecture I normally would have gotten. Even Gertie could tell I was feeling low. "Din-ner will be in an hour," she said. "Why don't you skip some rope until then?"

I stood around until Gertie was safely out of sight

before retrieving the stolen pen. First, I scouted up and down the block to make sure no one was around. In Canarsie, you don't just go sticking your hands down your pants for any reason.

The pen was broken. The plastic part split but it wasn't leaking. I really wished that, instead of shoving the pen down my pants, I could have dropped it down my blouse. In the movies, the floozy always folds up a ten spot and sticks it in her bra. Of course, if I had a bra I wouldn't have clipped the pen in the first place.

It really galled me to think that in order to see this doctor I missed *The Lavender Hill Mob* with Alec Guinness; something useful. Instead, I wasted my day with Dr. Know-Nothing.

I showed the pen to the super's mutt who wasn't very interested, so I stuck it in my pocket. One of the things I liked about that dog was he could tell when I didn't feel like playing. That is a rare quality in anyone. The decent mutt knew I wasn't up for tossing ball but I didn't feel like being alone either.

I remembered this movie I saw about a boy who ran off and joined the circus. It was called *Toby Tyler* which was also the name of the boy. Running off to join the circus would have solved some of my problems. I'd have fitted in at the circus. I asked the mutt if he wanted to come along. "We could work up an act," I said.

We might just have done that, too, except right then Gertie called down for me and broke up our plans.

■ ■ ■

38

I GATHERED Gertie had clued the rest of the family in beforehand on what a bust this doctor had been. No one mentioned it. Plus, they were all too nice to me. It wasn't normal.

The way I figured it, I might as well take advantage of this good nature toward me. "Is it okay if I watch the eight o'clock movie on television?" I asked over dinner.

Ordinarily, I could have counted on Gertie saying, "Absolutely not." Then she would have given me the tired story about how I watch far too much TV as is. And as long as I'm staring at a screen, why don't I watch something educational.

Herb also pushed educational television at me. One time he made me watch a show about a black kid who got lynched because he stole an apple. Herb wanted me to know that sort of thing does happen even in America.

Of course, having seen *To Kill a Mockingbird* and *They Won't Forget*, I already knew that. I told Herb as much but he said, "This is real. Not movie junk. Now, watch."

The night of the doctor, however, was different. I knew that I had them feeling sorry for me, and I could get away with most anything. "Just this once," Gertie said, "won't hurt."

The movie was *The River's Edge*, a better than average flick which starred Anthony Quinn and Ray Milland, a pair of real heavies.

I thought Herb might enjoy watching the movie with

me. I invited him and he said yes, which was sort of sweet of my father who usually didn't bother with me much. Only halfway into the movie, he got bored and buried his nose in the newspaper.

At ten o'clock sharp, Gertie came in and turned off the TV. "Time for bed," she said and sent me, and everyone else, to our rooms.

When I undressed, the stolen pen fell from my pocket. I put it on my night stand and got into my pajamas. But I had no intentions of going to sleep. Not when *Anatomy of a Murder* was on the late show.

To pass the hour until eleven o'clock, I took the pen and put it in an envelope. I sealed it shut using Scotch tape. Just for a goof, in red ink, I marked the envelope "Exhibit A" and put it in the left-hand bottom drawer of my desk.

And I promptly forgot all about it. I didn't remember Exhibit A until there was an Exhibit B to go with it.

ANY HOPES I might've had for ninth grade being an improvement over eighth grade were dashed by the third period on the very first day. For English, I got the Bat-Lady. Her other name was Mrs. Margolis but no one ever called her that. Except, of course, to her face. There were stories floating around about how she'd been dead for hundreds of years, about how she came back only to torture ninth graders. The Bat-Lady was no Miss Crabtree, the sweet and lovely teacher The Little Rascals had.

During roll call, we were required to sit up straight with our hands folded on our desks. When your name was called you had to say, "Present, Mrs. Margolis," if you were there. If you were absent, you needed a note from the President of the United States.

The Bat-Lady had a long list of rules for us. "Be advised," she said, "that in this class, spelling counts. I take off five points for each misspelled word." She foamed at the mouth over that idea. "Neatness," she went on, "does make a difference. I place great importance on fine penmanship."

I was doomed. Sunk. Spelling and neatness were my two worst subjects. With nothing left to lose, I raised my hand.

The Bat-Lady peered down at me over the tops of her halved glasses, the sort made exclusively for looking down at people. "You are?" she asked.

"Audrey," I said.

"Audrey? Audrey who? Audrey Audrey? You do not have a surname?"

"Feldman. Audrey Feldman."

"Feldman. Feldman," she was trying to place the name and I knew why. It was no surprise when she asked, "Are you Alexander Feldman's sister?"

Teachers always asked me that question with the same hopeful voice. Teachers and parents were the two groups who believed Alex was a prize.

I was expected to live up to Alex's reputation in the classroom. As a result, I looked worse than I was. A compounded disappointment was what I turned out to be.

"Alexander Feldman!" The Bat-Lady glowed with the memory of Alex volunteering to empty her trashcans. "Your brother," she said, "was a gem. I can only hope you are half the student he was."

"That's about it," I muttered. "Half."

Luckily, the Bat-Lady was too caught up with her pictures of Alex washing her blackboards and winning the city-wide Spelling Bee to have heard me. It took her a minute to snap out of it. "Excuse me," she said. "You had a question, I believe."

"More of a comment," I told her. "About the spelling and handwriting stuff."

"Stuff?" she asked.

"I don't think neatness should count," I said.

The Bat-Lady's face darkened. "A neat paper makes for a good impression. It says something about the work which went into it."

I totally disagreed with the Bat-Lady on that. "Judging us by our appearance is against the law," I said. "A good handwriting is something you're born with. The same as a pretty face or the color of your skin. Our handwritings are as different as our fingerprints." I got that from an old *Dragnet* episode so I was pretty sure it was true. "A person," I went on, "cannot change their handwriting so they shouldn't get points off if it's not one you happen to like. In other cultures," I said, "sloppy handwritings are worshiped." That one I'd made up on the spot but I thought it had a nice ring to it.

At that, Sharon Kessler's hand flew up in the air faster than a speeding bullet. "If you take time and care," she said, "then even poor handwriting can look presentable."

I shot Sharon Kessler, that twinkie, a look which was equal to one of the Black Hand's. Only Sharon Kessler was too busy gloating to notice.

"Well," I said.

"Well?" said the Bat-Lady. "Wells are water holes."

"Yes," I said. "But again, even spelling is a talent and some of us are lousy at it."

The Bat-Lady, I took note, was no longer listening to me. She was tapping her foot, waiting for me to be done. When I did finish, all she had to say was, "I can see you're nothing like your brother." If the Bat-Lady thought that remark was going to wound me in any way, she was mistaken.

The pity here was that I got saddled with the Bat-Lady for what was my best subject. As a rule, I did well in English classes. Mostly, that had a lot to do with the books or plays we had to read being based on movies I'd seen.

The movies gave me more to go on than the other kids had. "Good insights," teachers wrote on my papers. Also, seeing the movies made me remember details better. Once in a while, though, I did slip up.

One time we had to write a report on *Julius Caesar* and by mistake I kept calling Brutus James Mason. The name "James Mason" never showed up in the play but he was the lead in the movie of *Julius Caesar*.

Sometimes, if I liked a movie enough, I'd go so far as to read the book even if it wasn't assigned. The books weren't half bad, but they never measured up to the big screen.

I suspected, and I turned out to be right, that the Bat-Lady wasn't going to be the least bit interested in my additional insights. From that very first class, I was on her hit list. And the Bat-Lady was about as forgiving as Al Capone on St. Valentine's Day.

44

■ ■ ■

THE ONE thing I did learn on my first day of ninth grade was you can change schools but you can't change lunch rooms. The layout and makeup of a school cafeteria is a constant. In all schools, lunch tables are owned. Groups and teams and cliques have claimed them, and no matter which school you go to, one table always belongs to the cheerleaders and another one, usually right next to it, belongs to the football team. The debating team has their lunch table. And so on.

In Canarsie, there were several tables reserved for the kids who came to school with knives.

Lunch time can be a grim reminder each day that you don't belong to any of those tables. Lunch time can be an hour spent feeling very sorry for yourself and with good reason. The best you can hope for is that you blend into the walls and that no one notices you while you try to eat your sandwich which, a lot of the time, doesn't always go down easily because of the lump in your throat.

I knew the choices before me. One of the picks I had was to sit at the rejects' table with the kids who smelled like tuna fish, girls who were balding, boys with pitted skin. Rejects banded together because there was a safety in numbers.

To sit at their table, even just once on that first day of school, would have meant sitting there forever. Like being branded.

The other choice I had was to sit at one of the empty

tables by myself. In other words, proclaim to the entire world that I had no friends.

I may have been pathetic in some people's eyes but I wasn't pathetic enough to go with either of those choices. Instead, I made up a third one and ducked out of school.

No teacher stopped me. I just walked out and kept on going.

Maybe two blocks away, there was a patch of grass with a bench bolted in the center. In Brooklyn, this is called a park. That park was where I spent my lunch hour.

It was easy, there on the bench, away from everyone, to convince myself that eating outdoors was what I'd wanted to do all along. It was like Italy from what I knew of Italy from the movies, this eating outside.

Also, away from everyone it was easier not to face the music; that little tune about how since Rosalie moved away, no one had come to take her place.

I opened the brown paper bag Gertie had packed for me. Once again, I was very glad I had come to the park to eat. Gertie had made me a meatloaf sandwich. Also, she packed a banana. That was not the sort of lunch you wanted other people to know you ate.

I gave myself ten minutes to walk back to school. Along the way, I devised an alibi. The movies taught me that—always have an alibi handy. I decided I'd say I had felt dizzy and needed a breath of fresh air. If I got caught, that is. That was an excuse used in a ton of movies. Usually, it was by a woman with a boyfriend hiding in the yard. She would say to her husband, who was planted in a chair reading the paper, "I feel a little dizzy. I think I'll get some fresh air. Don't wait up for me, dear."

FOR SEVEN school days running, lunch in the park went without a hitch. Living by my wits, I managed to slip out of school and return undetected by students, teachers, or the screws. Even though I knew it wasn't exactly the same thing as *Escape From Alcatraz*, sometimes, in my head, I'd pretend that I'd outsmarted guards, that I'd made the great leap to freedom. I knew this was goofy but I figured it was okay to be goofy as long as no one saw it.

At the end of the second week, on a Friday, it rained. When I slipped out the door, the sky was clear and blue. There I was sitting on my bench eating an egg salad sandwich when clouds formed and burst all at once. It was just like that movie with Burt Lancaster, *The Rainmaker*. Torrents of rain fell on me and my lunch. My sandwich got washed away and I made a run for cover.

I ducked into the first open doorway, and there it was. I felt as if I'd stumbled onto the movie set of *The Hustler*, which starred Jackie Gleason and Paul Newman. I rubbed my eyes to make sure I wasn't seeing things, because this was too good to be true. I was afraid to move for fear it would go poof! and vanish. Also, I was afraid I'd get noticed and booted out.

There were six pool tables, real pool tables. Men,

haloed in smoke, crowded around two of them. This was the coolest place I'd ever been in. In real life, that is.

From *The Hustler*, I knew pool was very serious business. The men who played pool were not like the men who played ping pong. Often in a game of pool oodles of money was at stake.

I very carefully pulled a stool up to one of the tables. This one guy was hitting pockets like crazy. Those balls were ricocheting around that pool table like the silver ball in a pinball machine. Only these balls dropped into the pockets which the guy called. This man was lightning with a cue stick.

When he was down to two balls, the white one and the black one with the eight on it, he turned to me and said, "Don't move, kid. You're my Lady Luck."

Lady Luck. Like a real doll in the movies, I was a gambler's Lady Luck.

Just the idea of it made me so lightheaded, I nearly fell off the stool. When that eight-ball landed in the left corner pocket, just like he said it would, I clapped my hands.

The guy collected his dough from the loser and said to me, "Stick around, kid. I've got another game coming up in a minute." He told me his name was Tony. He was wearing blue jeans and a tee-shirt with a pack of Camels rolled up in the sleeve. He had dark hair and dark eyes and could have been a movie star easily.

I told him my name and he said, "Yeah. Well, you'll always be Lady Luck to me." Then he asked, "You want a beer or something, kid?"

Tony guided me over to the counter and told the

man standing behind it to get us two beers. I watched the man very closely to make sure he wasn't slipping me a Mickey Finn. But he was clean. He twisted off the caps of two Miller bottles. Tony handed one to me.

We clinked bottle heads and a hundred movie clips passed before me. Vivien Leigh catching sight of Clark Gable in *Gone With the Wind*, Bette Davis and Paul Henreid on the deck of an ocean liner under a full moon in *Now, Voyager*, Emil Jannings crowing for Marlene Dietrich in *The Blue Angel*. I, too, was in love.

Tony downed his beer in two gulps and ordered another one. I'd only taken a sip of mine. The truth was, I didn't like the taste very much. It reminded me of bad breath. The next time around, I decided to order one of those fancy drinks garnished with a cherry and a paper umbrella.

With sweaty palms I clutched at the beer bottle while Tony racked up for his next game. I was nervous but it turned out to be for nothing. Tony couldn't miss. Not with me there. He cleared the table in no time flat.

As he sank his last ball, I looked up at the clock on the wall. It was a dirty clock and fly-specked, just like it was supposed to be. It had class.

I was floating so high from this turn of events, I wasn't the least bit concerned that already I was fifteen minutes late getting back to school.

I said good-bye to Tony who was chalking his cue stick. "Yeah," he said. "So long, kid."

"See you around?" I asked.

And Tony said the magic word. "Sure," he said.

I took my beer with me when I left. I stepped outside to find the rain had passed. My eyes, adjusting from the darkened pool hall, hurt in the sun. Bending over the sewer, I poured the rest of my beer out. I was keeping the bottle though. I put it in my pocketbook. The empty Miller bottle nestled in between some candy wrappers and a history quiz.

BATS ARE supposed to be blind. Too bad for me the Bat-Lady was the exception to that rule. If anything, she must have had X-ray vision. As I entered through the fire exit, the Bat-Lady came flying around the corner and swooped down on me. "Where are you coming from?" she asked.

"I needed some air," I said. "I was dizzy and needed a breath of fresh air."

"You're all wet," she said. I corrected her and told her I was only a little damp.

The Bat-Lady must have thought she was Sherlock Holmes making deductions based on evidence. "The rain let up an hour ago," she said. "You've been out all that time. You stay after school today," she said. "With me. One half hour to make up for the class time you've missed and another hour as punishment for lying and leaving the school building without permission."

This was not possible for me to do. *Sorry, Wrong Number* was playing at the Variety that afternoon and I could not miss it. Not when Mr. Eisenstein brought it in especially for me. I had seen it before, but on television. Mr. Eisenstein said that was almost like not seeing it at all. "You have to see it on the big screen," he said, "to get the full impact."

"Be in my room at two-forty-five sharp!" The Bat-Lady wagged a pink claw at me.

"I'm sorry," I said, "but I can't do that." Because *Sorry, Wrong Number* was already on my mind, I simply lifted my excuse from the script. "My mother is an invalid," I said. "She needs me to come home straight from school. She's paralyzed, only the doctors don't know what's wrong. And we think my father might be trying to do her in. I have to be there to see to it nothing happens to her."

Perhaps I did get a little carried away there. What is perfectly believable in the movies does not always wash in real life. Still, I could see the Bat-Lady calculating the consequences of her keeping me after school while my old man did in my sickly mother. "Get to class, Audrey," the Bat-Lady said.

Sorry, Wrong Number on the big screen was well worth any lie I had to cook up in order to see it. "Didn't I tell you," Mr. Eisenstein said after it was over, "what a difference it makes? Television—" he made a face—"it makes everything little."

When I got home, Gertie asked, as she did every day, "So, what did you do this afternoon?"

"I was at the library," I replied.

Gertie smiled and told me, "Dinner is in fifteen

minutes. Go wash up. You don't know who was touching the books before you. They could have left germs on them."

In the bathroom, I took my Miller bottle from my purse and rinsed it out. I patted it dry with a towel, taking care not to rub away the label.

I would have liked to have kept the bottle on my night stand where I could see it all the time. Still, even I had enough marbles left in my head to know Gertie would have gone wild if she saw a beer bottle, empty or not, on my night stand. She'd start asking a zillion questions and there'd be no way I could explain Tony and the pool hall to my mother. She would call Herb in and together they would forbid me to ever again go into "that awful place." "And stay away from those dirty men. You don't know what kind of weirdos they could be."

To tell Gertie I had merely found the bottle would have been even worse. "What's wrong with you?" she'd say. "You don't know who drank from that. It could be carrying malaria for all you know."

The only thing I could call my own was my desk. It was the only space Gertie didn't regularly paw around in. She was always going through my dresser and closet because a few years before, she had discovered I was reusing dirty underwear. No matter how long ago that was, Gertie wasn't one to forget a thing like that. She continued to check. My desk was the only safe spot for my Miller bottle. I put it in the bottom drawer and tucked it in with a paper blanket.

52

■ ■ ■

THE AFTERNOON at the pool hall was nearly as real to me as a movie. When I put my head on the pillow to go to sleep, I began to see it that way even. I saw Tony and me on a screen. We were in black and white. He was wearing a tuxedo and a top hat. I had on a satin gown. I watched us dance. We looked like Ginger Rogers and Fred Astaire. As I drifted into sleep, and the screen got fuzzy, we *were* Ginger Rogers and Fred Astaire.

OVER THE weekend, while I was catching a double bill of *The Thin Man* and *The Thin Man Goes Home*, the Bat-Lady must have been doing some detective work of her own.

First thing during Monday morning homeroom an announcement came over the loudspeaker. "Aud-rey *Feld-man*, pul-ease report to the prin-ci-pull's office. *At once*."

The walk to the principal's office was down a long corridor very much like James Cagney's walk down Death Row in *Angels With Dirty Faces*. A walk in slow motion. That is how everything looks and feels when you're in big trouble.

Mr. Davis, the principal, was sitting at his desk. The Bat-Lady stood behind him.

"Audrey," she said in a sweet voice which didn't fool me any, "why don't you tell Mr. Davis about your invalid mother?"

54

"Excuse me," I said. "I'm afraid I don't understand."

"Tell him," she said, "what you told me when I caught you coming in the fire exit on Friday." The Bat-Lady thought she had me with my back to the wall. Too bad the Bat-Lady hadn't seen *All About Eve* as many times as I have. She didn't know about the merits of bold-faced lying. Nor did she know how to be cunning and devious. I'd practically memorized Anne Baxter's performance, which gave me an edge on playing innocent when guilty.

"Friday?" I cocked my head. "I don't believe we spoke on Friday, Mrs. Margolis. Except, of course, in class when you asked me to diagram a sentence."

"After that," she said. "After lunch. And I told you that you'd have to stay after school for leaving the building. And you said you could not because your mother was an invalid."

I told the Bat-Lady she must have mixed me up with someone else. "Maybe you need a vacation, Mrs. Margolis," I said, even though she'd just had the whole summer off.

Mr. Davis said nothing but kept looking from the Bat-Lady to me and back to her like he was watching a tennis match.

The Bat-Lady looked like she might go mad. The veins in her neck got big the way my father's did when he got furious. Only the Bat-Lady's stood out even more. I never saw anyone so angry in my life. It was sort of interesting.

My tragic flaw, which Mr. Eisenstein once explained to me all dramatic heroines have—which is

55

why a lot of movies don't have happy endings—was that I didn't know when to quit. I should have been satisfied in just making the Bat-Lady a little crazy. Instead, I continued, "Maybe you'd better call the guys with the white coats, Mr. Davis. She looks insane to me, don't you agree?"

Mr. Davis couldn't let me get away with saying that to a teacher. The way he phrased it, "You don't leave me any choice, Audrey." He sentenced me to a month's worth of detention. Hard labor. "Ninety minutes a day, young lady," he said, "with Mrs. Margolis."

The Bat-Lady didn't think that was punishment enough. She wanted me to work the rock pile every day for the next ten years.

The way I figured it, a month or ten years was all the same. It was torture. They might as well have told me I couldn't breathe for a month. Missing out on a month of movies, I'd dry up. I'd perish.

This wasn't just any old month of movies, either. Mr. Eisenstein was bringing in a four-star line-up: *Garden of Evil* with Susan Hayward, Gary Cooper, and Richard Widmark, one of the great heavies; *Cover-Up*; *Studs Lonigan*; and *Treasure of the Sierra Madre*, which I'd never seen due to the fact that the last time Mr. Eisenstein showed it, I had a fever of 102.5 and Gertie wouldn't let me go. I couldn't miss it again. It was a Bogart movie.

They had me cornered. I asked the Bat-Lady if she wouldn't rather flog me instead. For a minute there, I thought she'd go for that but she said, "A month of detentions. You heard Mr. Davis."

I needed help to get out of this. Unfortunately, this wasn't one of those times I could ask Gertie. She would never have taken my word over a teacher's. Besides, she'd never agree to come plead my case in a wheel-chair.

During algebra, I came up with the answer. Tony was my ace in the hole. Didn't he practically say to me, "If you need me, just whistle. You do know how to whistle, don't you?" Actually, that was Lauren Bacall who said that. She said it to Bogart in *To Have and Have Not*. But it might as well have been Tony saying it to me. He implied it. I was his Lady Luck. The way I figured it, he'd stare the Bat-Lady down and tell her it was impossible for me to stay after school. "And why not?" the Bat-Lady would say.

"Because I say so," would be Tony's answer and the Bat-Lady would quake in her boots.

I wasted no time, once the lunch bell rang, in getting to the pool hall. I burst through the doors like six-guns blazing at the OK Corral.

Tony was hunched over the third pool table from the door, a cigarette dangling from his lips. He smoked it without touching it. Muscles showed through his tee-shirt. Definitely another Brando. Or James Dean. He was lined up for a shot when I tapped him on the shoulder. "It's me," I said. "Lady Luck."

The white ball bounced on the felt but none of the balls went in any of the holes. Tony swung around. "Beat it, kid," he said. "You just made me scratch."

"Don't you remember me?" I asked. "From Friday? I was your Lady Luck on Friday."

"Well, you're bad luck now. So get lost." He turned his back on me.

My face grew hot. No doubt it was red like a tomato. What a creep. He was probably one of those weirdo perverts Gertie was always warning me about. "Two-bit pool hustler," I yelled.

On my way out the door, I grabbed a block of blue chalk. It wasn't anything special. It was just a square of chalk with a round indentation in the center where it met up with a cue stick again and again.

I sat myself on my park bench and tore out a piece of notebook paper which I used to wrap the chalk in so it wouldn't get dust all over. In small print, I wrote on the paper, "Exhibit B," and dropped it in my pocketbook.

0 9 8 7 6

THE FIRST afternoon of detention, the Bat-Lady sat me down at a front row desk and stood over me. Her fangs glistened. She told me I was to write, "I will not tell lies," five hundred times.

I said, "You've got to be kidding," and then went on to suggest to her that such punishment served no purpose. "Wouldn't it be more constructive," I asked, "if we had me write an essay questioning the morality of minor untruths? To be honest," I told her, "I am certain I'll tell lies again. Everyone tells lies sometimes. There are circumstances. No one is always honest," I said.

"Make that one thousand times," was the Bat-Lady's reply. "I will not tell lies. One thousand times. I suggest you get started."

I wrote, "I will not tell lies," until I thought my hand was going to fall off. I got two blisters from that, one on the joint of my middle finger and the other on the tip of my thumb. And I got to thinking that these blisters could burst and get infected and then gangrened and they'd have to amputate and it would all be the Bat-Lady's doing.

I was rubbing them where they hurt when she swooped down on me. She picked the papers up off my desk and peered at them. "I'm not done yet," I told her.

"This will do," the Bat-Lady said just as, right before my very eyes, she tore my papers in half and then into quarters and dropped them in the trash. I don't know what I expected her to do with them, but still, to drop my efforts in the garbage seemed very cruel. She could have at least looked them over for spelling.

The way I saw it, the Bat-Lady must have been a regular at *Horror Hotel*. The following day, she actually made me sit there and twiddle my thumbs, while *The Lady from Shanghai* was playing at the Variety. Honest.

"Twiddle your thumbs," she said when I asked her what she wanted of me today. I was surprised she didn't stick bamboo shoots up under the fingernails before ordering me to twiddle.

On what should have been my fifth detention in a row, a Friday, I lit out and went to the movies instead. I had to do this. *North by Northwest* was showing. I was not about to miss one of Alfred Hitchcock's best just so the Bat-Lady could go on with her games.

I got to the Variety at my usual time. Mr. Eisenstein was in the lobby looking quite natty in his blue suit even if it was shiny around the elbows. He wore a diamond chip tie tac. Mr. Eisenstein dressed up for Cary Grant movies. He told me he did that because, "My old friend Cary Grant is a very classy fellow." Mr. Eisenstein called Cary Grant "my old friend" even though I was certain Cary Grant wouldn't know Mr. Eisenstein if they collided head on. But I knew what he meant when he called him "my old friend." Mr. Eisenstein also called Marlene Dietrich "my old flame" like they really had danced the tango together. The people on the screen could be your best friends even if they'd never heard of you.

"So," Mr. Eisenstein said to me, "you came to see my old friend Cary Grant. So, where were you the rest of the week? You missed some of the greats, Audrey. Three out of four were Academy Award winners. And those were the days when the Academy meant something."

Without giving too many details, I sort of explained my situation to Mr. Eisenstein. "This teacher," I said, "really doesn't like me. She's making me stay after school every day for a month." I left out the part about my lying because I didn't want Mr. Eisenstein to know that about me.

"A month," Mr. Eisenstein said, "sounds very serious. What could you have done to deserve such punishment?"

"Nothing," I said. "I was framed and sent up the river."

Mr. Eisenstein had seen enough movies to know

that people really do get framed. "A month," he repeated, shaking his head. "What a shame. Such a month I have coming up, Audrey. Never mind what you missed this week already. You can't ask the lady nicely to let you out?"

I asked Mr. Eisenstein if he remembered *The Maltese Falcon*.

"I'm familiar with the film, yes," he said, sort of on the sarcastic side, which I understood. He must have seen *The Maltese Falcon* so many times, he practically was in it.

"Well," I said, "remember how Mary Astor begs Humphrey Bogart to show her some mercy? And for that minute there, you think he might let her go free even if she is a murderess? But not old Bogart. He was hard as nails and he turned her in. She didn't have a chance in the world even though she asked nicely."

"I see," Mr. Eisenstein said. "Well, Audrey. One of the beauties of the movies is they are on film. Celluloid isn't going anywhere. For now, you go inside and get comfortable to watch my old friend Cary Grant in *North by Northwest*."

On Saturday, I saw *Harvey* at the Variety. *Harvey* is a nice, nice movie which melted away my worries like gumdrops. Harvey is this giant white rabbit that only Jimmy Stewart can see. It made me feel like I had a secret friend, too. The part at the end, when Harvey follows Jimmy Stewart through the door, was a kicker. It made me feel so good, I actually forgot how bleak my situation was.

Tough luck for me, the Bat-Lady did not see *Harvey*

on Saturday. Or at any other time, most likely. She didn't forget my bleak situation and worse, she did not forget that I pulled a no-show on Friday.

During homeroom, she escorted me out into the hallway and demanded an explanation. "Where were you on Friday?" she hissed.

I did not tell a lie. "I went to the movies," I said, expecting to be rewarded for my honesty, if nothing else. The way I figured it, she should've been pleased that I told the truth.

But she seemed to take no notice of that. "The movies," she said. "How dare you? Where did you get the nerve to go to the movies when we had an appointment?"

"Because," I said, "*North by Northwest* was playing."

"*North by Northwest*," the Bat-Lady echoed me, only she sounded like she didn't know what we were talking about.

I tried filling her in, telling her how it was one of Hitchcock's finest. "With Cary Grant," I said. "It's a suspense movie only sometimes it's funny, too. It's the one that features Mt. Rushmore, which I learned about in history class but finally got to see in real life."

"I know the movie," the Bat-Lady said.

"Then you understand why I had to see it." I turned out to be dead wrong.

All she understood was that I disobeyed her for which she added on two additional weeks to the three left of my prison sentence. Five more weeks all totaled.

Telling the truth gets you in as much trouble as

telling lies. The real trick, the way I figured it, was to plead the fifth on all accounts: I cannot answer on the grounds it could incriminate me.

That afternoon, she had me cleaning the erasers. That meant taking one in each hand and pounding them together like I was doing bust-development exercises. Maybe it wasn't a total loss, in that regard. Still, each time I clapped the erasers together, a cloud of chalk dust flew in my face. Plus, I was missing *Cover-up*.

All that chalk dust had to be dangerous to my health. I could have gotten some respiratory disease and then I'd have to go to the hospital and get hooked up to an iron lung. The Bat-Lady would have to come to the hospital then and stand over my sick, limp, weak little body. She would have to beg for my forgiveness. She'd have to say, "I didn't mean you any harm, kid. You gotta believe me." I'd look at her, too tired to respond and that would be the end. The credits would come up and the audience would never know if I forgave her or not. The way I figured it, they'd be rooting for me not to.

I looked up from the chalk dust and coughed a lot for effect but the Bat-Lady took no notice. She was hunched over her desk filling in her grade book. Every couple of notations, she'd switch pens, putting down her blue pen and hungrily reaching for the red one. It was obvious the Bat-Lady got a real charge from using that red pen. The red pen stood for our failures.

"Hey, Mrs. Margolis," I said.

She looked up like she'd just smelled something bad. "You weren't speaking to me, were you?" she asked.

"Yes, I was," I said. "Did you ever see a movie called *The Prime of Miss Jean Brodie?*" I asked. "Now, there was a school teacher with spunk. I caught that movie on television a couple of weeks ago. On the Midnight Movie. It was so inspiring the way Miss Brodie adored her students. It made me consider becoming a teacher."

"Do your parents know you stay up to watch television past midnight?" was all the Bat-Lady had to say about that.

"Oh, yes," I said. "They watched it with me. We're big movie fans at my house. Do you like the movies?" I asked.

"I fail to see the purpose of this conversation," the Bat-Lady said.

"There is no purpose," I said, which, of course, was yet another lie. "I was just wondering if you liked the movies, was all."

The Bat-Lady looked at me like I was losing my marbles, which made sense in a way. It did seem crazy making polite chit-chat with the enemy. But there was a method to my madness. That's from some movie, "Though this be madness, yet there is method in't." I forget which one but it starred Laurence Olivier and took place in the very olden days.

"You see," I said to the Bat-Lady, "the movies expand my horizons. I learn from them." I wanted her to think I saw educational movies.

"Audrey," she said, "movies are nothing but entertainment. And bad entertainment at that."

"Oh no, Mrs. Margolis," I said. "Movies are Art."

I didn't really know that for certain. I had always thought Art was paintings, but Mr. Eisenstein said movies were Art, too. I had no real reason to doubt him.

This also failed, however, to sway the Bat-Lady. Instead, she got up and inspected the erasers and told me they weren't clean enough.

At four-fifteen, she dismissed me. "You can go now," she said, but before I got out the door, she called me back. "Audrey, what time do your afternoon movies begin?"

"Four o'clock," I told her.

"And how long does it take you to get to the movie house from here?"

"Around fifteen minutes," I said.

"Then staying here every day until this time guarantees that you'll miss your movie?"

"Yes," I said, thinking the Bat-Lady was about to get softhearted on me.

"Good," she said. She was thrilled over the idea she was keeping me from the one thing that mattered.

I picked up my books again and maneuvered into my jacket which wasn't real black leather but looked a lot like it. The Bat-Lady stood at the door, her back to me, shutting off the lights. I grabbed her red pen off her desk and slipped it into my biology text. "Have a pleasant evening, Mrs. Margolis," I said. I felt a bit better knowing that I had robbed her of her one joy, too. We were even, sort of.

THE SUPER'S dog was on the steps waiting for me when I got home. His tail was wagging and his ears were pinned back with devotion. I patted him on the head, which got him so excited his whole bottom shook. The mutt was becoming my equivalent to Harvey the rabbit.

Gertie had never let me have a dog, or any pet for that matter. Her claim was that animals, and especially dogs, were dirty and who was going to clean up after them?

Nora Charles from "The Thin Man" movies had a dog whose name was Asta. Nora Charles was played by Myrna Loy, who was a very classy lady, and I don't think she would have had a dog if they were the way Gertie said.

I find dogs to be very nice creatures. For one thing, they don't judge you according to your size.

THE BAT-LADY'S pen went into the desk drawer along with the other stuff I'd lifted. At that time, my loot consisted of two pens and a block of pool-cue chalk. It wasn't anything they'd send me to Riker's Island over, but it was definitely a foreshadowing of things to come. Foreshadowing is a movie term which Mr. Eisenstein taught me. It means hints. Compared to later heists, my stash was, at that point, very small potatoes. But it was definitely foreshadowing.

Gertie yelled into my room that dinner was in twenty minutes. Gertie knew nothing of my detentions. As I was never home before six anyhow, there was no need for her to be on to anything.

Ruth came into the bedroom and sat next to me on the bed. "How's everything?" she asked.

I shrugged and Ruth said, "If something is bothering you, you know you can tell me."

I had already thought of this. I knew I needed the aid of a grown-up person to get me out of those detentions. Ruth wasn't exactly an adult but she was old enough to be my legal guardian. She could get me sprung.

Before spilling my guts, I made Ruth swear up and down and cross her heart that she would not rat on me. It hurt Ruth's feelings that I could not trust her outright but I wasn't about to take chances. Besides, on occasion Ruth had been known to snitch. Not because she was a dirty double-crosser like Alex, but because Ruth thought snitching was often for your own good, answering what she thought was a cry for a different kind of help.

"I promise," she said. "Cross my heart. Sugar on top." I didn't ask for the sugar. That was Ruth's personal contribution.

I told her the whole story of my hard luck, my downfall, my ruination. "Five more weeks of detention, Ruth. It's inhuman. I have no life left."

Ruth wanted to know exactly what lie I told the Bat-Lady which made her dish out such harsh punishment.

Before I'd tell her, I made Ruth renew her vows of silence.

"Audrey," Ruth said, "that's terrible. How could you tell such a horrid lie? Mother an invalid? How could you even think such a thing?"

"I was desperate, Ruth. *Sorry, Wrong Number* was

68

playing. I had to go to the movies. I simply had to. And the second time it was *North by Northwest*. These are great movies, Ruth."

"You know Mother doesn't want you going to the movies so often. Especially on school days. Didn't she forbid you to go to the movies on school days?"

"Ruth," I asked, "weren't you ever my age?"

Ruth got that hurt look on her puss again. "Of course I was," she said.

"So, didn't you ever do things you weren't supposed to do?"

Ruth had to think that over. In the end, she wasn't able to come up with a single act of disobedience. How did I land such a sister? I should have had one who went out dancing until the sun came up, a girl who returns home with her lipstick smeared.

"I do agree," Ruth said, "that six straight weeks of detention does seem a bit harsh."

"Then you'll go in there and spring me?" I asked.

"Pardon?" Ruth said. "Spring you? I don't understand."

She was hopeless but she was all I had. "Spring me, Ruth. Set me free. Talk some sense into Mrs. Margolis."

"Audrey," Ruth said, "she is the teacher and you'll just have to accept her decision."

I put on my victimized little-girl face and said, "She hates me, Ruth. She's got it in for me."

"Maybe she does," Ruth replied, "and I'm sorry about that. But it's a part of life. We have to learn how to get along with all sorts of people. You have to make an effort to make peace with your teacher. If that means playing by her rules, then that is what you have to do. Like it or not, that's how life is."

That may have been how Ruth saw life, but I wasn't about to play by some square's set of rules. The system can be bucked. Frank Capra's movies showed me that.

"In the movies," I said to Ruth, "the little guy can fight back and win. Did you ever see *Mr. Smith Goes to Washington?*"

"Audrey," Ruth said, "movies are not real life."

"You bet movies aren't real life," I said. "Movies are wonderful and I sure wish I was in one now."

When you're at the movies, sitting on a velvet seat in a dark theater, you can be in the movie if you want. They let you do that. They let you go right up there on the silver screen and join in, believing you are Rosalind Russell, ace reporter in *His Girl Friday*, or Edward G. Robinson's favorite moll. And even when the movie's over, you can stay up there. You can go on being that star on the screen until someone on the outside pulls the plug by reminding you to pick up your socks or do your homework or take out the garbage, or worst of all, telling you that movies aren't real life.

Ruth gave me the sermon about taking my lumps and coming out a better person for it. It was the same sermon the coppers give the crook when they want him to turn himself or his buddies in. A speech designed for suckers. Ruth was telling me to be the fall guy and not think twice about it. That might have been okay for her, but it was not okay for the likes of me.

As A LAST resort, I took Mr. Eisenstein's suggestion. Nicely and politely, I asked the Bat-Lady to reduce my sentence. "Is there such a thing around here as time off for good behavior?" I wanted to know. I might as well have asked Duffy of San Quentin to let me out of the Big House. "Absolutely not," the Bat-Lady said.

To MAKE UP for missing all those movies, television became my life-support system. Although the TV screen was too small to climb into and a lot of the movies shown on TV were junky, it beat cold turkey.

The downside to the TV alternative, aside from the second-rate viewing, was more spats with Gertie. Gertie was, in her own words, at wit's end with me.

"Every waking minute in front of the television," she yelled. Gertie was prone to exaggerate. There wasn't any TV at school and I did take time out to eat.

Actually, I tried to combine dining and viewing, but Gertie wasn't receptive to my request for snack tables.

"What?" she asked.

"Snack tables," I said. "Aluminum trays on collapsible legs you can set up anywhere but mostly in front of the television."

"I know what snack tables are," Gertie said. "Cannibals eat off of them. Cannibals watch television while having dinner. People eat dinner at the dinner table."

If Gertie wanted me to watch less television, she would have to bodily drag me off. As that wasn't Gertie's style, she called Herb in to talk to me instead. I heard her in the kitchen saying, "Talk to her, Herb. She hasn't moved from in front of that TV all night. She's in high school. Her grades count toward college and she's not even doing her homework. Go on. Talk to her."

So Herb came in to talk to me. I made him wait for the commercial because *Detective Story* was on. This was a rare TV treat. And Herb wanted to talk while Lee Grant was getting booked by Kirk Douglas. "In a minute," I said.

When the movie cut for a commercial I lowered the volume and said to Herb, "You've got sixty seconds. Shoot."

"Don't watch so much television," Herb said.

"Why not?" I asked.

"Because," Herb said. "Because" was one of those reasons my parents gave a lot. Sometimes they embellished it by adding, "Because I said so." "Because" is not a good reason and is not acceptable. I knew this from my science class when a question on a test read, "Why do plants need sunlight?" I wrote, "Because," and the teacher wrote back, "Not acceptable. F."

"Not an acceptable answer," I said to Herb. In turn, he told me to watch how I talked to my father.

"Why?" I asked.

"Because," Herb said.

The next thing I knew, we were having ourselves an Abbott and Costello routine. "Because why?" I asked.

"Because I said so," Herb said.

We could have gone on like that all night except the commercial was over and my attention turned back to Kirk Douglas. On top of the sound track, Herb called out, "Your mother doesn't want you watching so much television. It's bad for your eyes."

I assured Herb that my eyes were fine. "Still," he said, "you ought to go out and play more with the little girls your own age."

"Herb," I reminded him, "the girls my own age are no longer little."

"Don't call me Herb," he said.

"Why?"

"Because."

IN THE movies, when a con is about to be paroled, they always give him a new suit and a pair of shoes and ten bucks. Also, the warden gives him a pep talk. "Try to keep your nose clean, Johnny," the warden always says. This way, the con can start fresh.

As the last detention came to a close, I thought the Bat-Lady would play the role of the warden. I thought she'd tell me something like, "You're not such a rotten kid, Audrey. You had some bad breaks is all, but I think we both learned a few things. Good luck." I had this idea that we would shake hands.

I was mistaken. The Bat-Lady had no encouraging words for me. No new suit. No shoes. No ten bucks.

The clock neared four-fifteen and I got more than a little concerned that perhaps she didn't realize this was my last detention.

"Mrs. Margolis," I said finally, "you are aware that this is my last afternoon with you?"

"I know that," she said.

The Bat-Lady and I left the room together. All the way down the hall, I was still waiting for her to say something, even if it was only something Bat-like such as, "I hope this is the end of your lying." Only she wouldn't give me even that. She didn't think I was worth as much breath as any petty criminal. That hit me where I lived.

"Mrs. Margolis," I said, "I just remembered I left something in the room."

"So go get it." She continued down the hallway.

"But you locked the door," I said.

The Bat-Lady made a face, which wasn't the easiest thing to detect when you considered her mug wasn't too pretty to start out with.

It was obvious that Bat-Lady did not trust me with her keys. She walked me back down the hallway, complaining the whole way.

When you look back at the movie of your life, sometimes there's a frame or two where you know if just one thing had gone differently, the whole plot would have changed course. If the Bat-Lady had stayed put and given me the keys, if she had trusted me just that little bit, my life of crime probably would have ended then and there.

Instead, she walked me right up to the classroom door before fishing out her key ring. It was a brass key ring with about a thousand keys dangling from it. No doubt each one stood for a kid she had locked up someplace. "And make it fast." She opened the door.

I scooted into the classroom and clipped a blackboard eraser, dropping it into my pocketbook.

"Got it," I said.

"What did you leave in there that was so important?" The Bat-Lady wouldn't dream of minding her own business.

"My eraser," I said.

"We went all the way back for an eraser?" she asked.

"Not just any eraser," I told the Bat-Lady. "This one has sentimental value."

MR. EISENSTEIN treated me to a cherry soda as a "welcome back to the movies" present. We were sitting in the lobby of the Variety when, out of nowhere, he said, "Business is lousy, Audrey. I'm barely holding my own here. A Saturday matinee and look around." He made a sweeping gesture with one hand. "This should be my busiest day and maybe, if I'm lucky, I've sold fourteen tickets."

I didn't like hearing that Mr. Eisenstein had any problems. "Well," I said, "what can you do?"

"What can I do?" he repeated. "You mentioned once I could show first-run movies. I could turn the Variety into Cinema One Two Three Four Five Six Seven. That's what I could do."

The thought of that made me lose my appetite. I put down my soda. "But what about Sergei Eisenstein? You can't do that to Sergei. You wouldn't!"

"Well, I certainly don't want to if that's what you mean. But as it is, I can barely keep us in popcorn. However, I've got one last trick up my sleeve. A festival," he said. "The revival houses across the bridge are always having festivals and they do a million dollars worth of business." "Across the bridge" was what Mr. Eisenstein called Manhattan.

"Those theatres," he went on, "don't do anything different from what I do. Only they give it a name. They show a week of Judy Garland movies and call it a Judy Garland Festival and bingo! it's an event and everyone is knocking down the doors to get in. So, do you think maybe a festival would go over big in Canarsie?"

"Yeah," I said. "I get it." I stood up and did a bump and a grind and cracked, "You gotta have a gimmick, right?"

Mr. Eisenstein looked at me like he didn't have a clue as to what I was talking about, but I knew he did. It was only the Saturday before that I'd seen *Gypsy* in his theatre.

"Remember," I said. "Natalie Wood? Rosalind Russell? Karl Malden? That's from the song the strippers sang to Natalie Wood when she was first getting started in professional life. 'You Gotta Have a Gimmick.' "

"Oh," said Mr. Eisenstein. "I didn't recognize it without the equipment." I quickly sat down again. Mr. Eisenstein would never have made a remark like that intentionally but still, it sounded to me like a direct jab about my size.

"What I meant," he said, "is there weren't any lights. Or feathers. Or fans. And that one had a bugle. You weren't holding a bugle so I didn't recognize the song."

Mr. Eisenstein came up with the idea of a 3-D Festival. "Three dimensional movies," he told me, "never really took off. They thought it would be the new wave of the future in film," he said. "Like talkies. Only talkies caught on."

According to him, all the 3-D movies ever made were pure junk because they were made for the special effects alone. "No story lines. Lousy acting. They died." However, as Mr. Eisenstein figured it, 3-D would make for a catchy festival. "Like you said, Audrey. A gimmick."

He got three 3-D movies for the coming Saturday. "Three 3-D," he said. "Get it? It's keeping to a theme." He took out a full-page ad in the local paper. The movies were scheduled to begin at noon and run until 6:00 P.M. with two intermissions. That way people could buy more popcorn and still not miss anything.

Mr. Eisenstein said he was going to charge an extra fifty cents admission but throw in the 3-D glasses for free. 3-D glasses are not real glasses the way 3-D glasses are advertised on backs of comic books. They're flimsy cardboard wrap-around jobs.

I got there a half an hour early and found the Variety in its usual state. Empty except for Mr. Eisenstein and two or three of the other regulars. I was waiting to have my pre-movie yak with him, when they started coming.

The lobby began filling up, and not just with regular people. Kids from my school were coming in. When Mr. Eisenstein said he wanted to increase business, I had no idea he meant like that.

"Audrey—" he found his way to me—"go in and get a good seat now. Looks like we'll have a full house."

I took the front row aisle seat. That was the least desirable seat in the theatre but, considering its position, my best shot at not being spotted. For double incognito purposes, I put on the cardboard shades. I most definitely did not want to be recognized by my classmates, who by then were pouring in by twos and threes. It seemed as if everyone who came to the Variety that day was with a boyfriend or their lunch-table crowd. I was the only person in the world alone at the movies. I slunk way down in the seat.

As the Variety was filling to the rafters, I realized I was about to have company. Even the front row, where you can always bank on solitude, was about to become occupied. I could only hope for some little old lady next to me.

Instead, I got Elinore Ditmar and that growth on her arm otherwise known as Ricky Weiss. Elinore took the seat directly next to mine. I shielded my face and turned the other way but that Elinore Ditmar was a quick cookie. She didn't miss a trick. "Look, Ricky," she said, "it's Audrey. Audrey Feldman, isn't that you?"

"Very sharp," I said.

"Whatever are you doing here?" Elinore wanted to

know, as if it were her movie house and I was the intruder.

I was about to tell her I was here for the same reason she was, but then I saw that maybe we weren't there for the same reasons. Ricky Weiss was sort of panting. "I'm here to see the movies," I said. "What else?"

Elinore giggled and Ricky snorted. "But who with?" Elinore asked. "Who are you here with?"

"Myself," I said, trying very hard to make that not sound as pathetic as it was.

"You came to the movies by yourself?" Elinore Ditmar squealed. "How queer. Isn't that queer, Ricky?"

Ricky thought it was queer, too.

The house lights went dark and I turned my attention to the screen. I heard Elinore Ditmar say, "Ricky, I'm scared." What a twinkie. The girl was scared and the movie hadn't even begun. I hoped she wasn't going to talk all through it. There's nothing worse than a yakker in the theatre.

The first movie was *House of Wax*. Elinore shrieked at the credits. Ricky moved closer to protect her. They were crowding me. I would have asked them if they wanted me to get up so they could stretch out except I was pretty certain they would have said yes.

Elinore Ditmar and Ricky Weiss were not the only ones ruining the movie for me. I'd thought the audience at a movie festival would be other movie fans, not kids from my school who knew nothing about movie-going. These people were there to talk or kiss and some guys in the balcony were actually throwing popcorn. They weren't here for the movies at all.

During a lull in *House of Wax*, I started watching Ricky Weiss try to cop a feel off of Elinore Ditmar. I didn't mean to be watching. It was just that the movie on the screen was going a little slow, so I got caught up in the action next to me instead. It might have made for a good show if Elinore didn't suddenly open her eyes and say, "What are you looking at, you little creep? She was staring at us, Ricky. The little creep was getting off watching us."

Ricky called me a little creep, too.

In the middle of *The Charge at Feather River*, right after the cowboy spit tobacco juice at us, I decided to leave. The special effects had begun to wear thin. Once you've seen hot wax poured from the screen or an arrow shot straight at you a couple of times what's a dozen more of the same gimmick?

The last thing I wanted to hear that afternoon was the gang talk about where they were going next as if they were all Judy Garland and Mickey Rooney in an Andy Hardy movie. I didn't want to overhear plans for Saturday night, and most of all, I did not want to hear anyone else say, "Audrey, who are you here with?" So I gathered up my belongings and made a quick getaway while a tomahawk was being hurled.

Mr. Eisenstein was not in the lobby. He must have been in his office counting up his loot. Even though I knew it was a lousy thing to wish, I couldn't help but hope business at the Variety wouldn't be so good ever again. I dumped the flimsy 3-D glasses in the trash.

Not wanting to hang around the Variety for a minute

longer, I waited until I hit the street before I put on my jacket. My pocketbook held between my teeth, I had slipped in one arm when I saw something bright fall to the ground. I bent over and picked up a purple hat. One of those beret hats. It wasn't mine.

I dusted off the purple beret. I knew I'd seen it before and then I remembered where. I'd seen it on Elinore Ditmar's head. It must have fallen off during one of her passionate moments with Ricky Weiss and landed on my jacket. I'd scooped it up by mistake.

For a foolish, soft-hearted minute, I thought about going back in and returning the purple beret to Elinore Ditmar. I pictured the scene this way: Elinore would be sick with grief over losing her favorite hat. She loved that hat. Maybe Ricky had bought it for her. They would be ripping the seats apart looking for it when I'd make my entrance. Elinore would weep with joy over getting her hat back. "How can I ever thank you enough?" she'd say. For starters, she and Rickey would ask me to join them after the movie for a pizza and a soda. That was my first version of the scene.

The second version was more true to life. I saw that the first version wouldn't happen even in the sloppiest moments of the gushiest tear-jerker. What would happen, if I went back inside the Variety, was Elinore Ditmar would see me holding her hat before I could even tell her it was an accident, and she would point a finger at me and shriek, "You stole my hat."

So that's what I did. I stole her hat.

Finders keepers.

82

I rolled the purple beret into a ball and stuffed it in my pocket. Keeping my face down, I walked home briskly.

The super's dog wasn't on the steps so I headed directly upstairs. I called out for Gertie but got no answer. She must have been at the market or over at one of the neighbor's. Herb was at the office putting in overtime. Ruth was still at the library, and Alex must have been at the lot playing stickball. It was a rare coming together of the forces that found me home alone. I decided to enjoy it even though I sort of did want some company.

I settled in my bedroom where I filed the beret in with the rest of my loot. It might have commanded a ten spot brand new but I didn't think a hat was the sort of thing I could fence. My loot, the way I figured it, had a different sort of value: satisfaction.

I thought about the victims when they discovered their goods were missing. I wondered if I was their prime suspect—or was I above suspicion? "Not that sweet little girl," I pictured them saying.

Of course, if all my easy marks gathered together in one room and asked the same questions, they could have stumbled onto a pattern. I killed the better part of the next hour pretending to be Basil Rathbone as Sherlock Holmes and tried to figure out my own crimes.

It was fun until I heard Alex come in the door. I knew it was Alex because I heard him wiping his feet on the mat. Alex was such a twinkie. He was such a good boy. Such a potential blabber-mouthed rat. I quickly wrapped up my loot and put it back in the desk drawer a.k.a. "the safe"; a.k.a. stands for "also known as." Most criminals and gangsters have an a.k.a. It comes with the territory.

ONCE EVERY three months we went for a Sunday visit to my Aunt Ida, Herb's older sister. This was before Aunt Ida went to live at a retirement village in Florida. For these occasions, Gertie always took her mink stole out of storage. Gertie wore that mink whenever we went to Aunt Ida's no matter what the weather was. This was because Aunt Ida didn't have a mink stole.

"She likes so much to look at mine," Gertie said. "I would hate to disappoint her by not wearing it."

Going to Aunt Ida's was not something we ever wanted to do. We all had better ways to spend that day. "Aunt Ida looks forward to this," Gertie always said. "She loves having us. You can give up one afternoon for Aunt Ida's sake."

The way I figured it, Aunt Ida wanted us to come for dinner as much as she liked having her nose rubbed in Gertie's fur stole.

To get to her house, we had to drive through a tough neighborhood, the sort I was very familiar with from the movies. Gertie and Herb called that neighborhood "a ghetto" and Ruth called it "underprivileged."

Whenever we approached the border—marked by a row of burned-out buildings—Gertie, on cue, swung around and said, "Children, are your doors locked? Lock your doors." I didn't have a clue as to what Gertie thought would happen if we drove through a rough neighborhood without locking the car doors. Did she think a thug would run up to our station wagon, wrench a door open and pull one of us out? To do what with us, I had no idea. I was hardly worth pawing over and Alex isn't worth two cents. Even Gertie's mink, which might have been good enough to make Aunt Ida jealous, was old. No self-respecting fence would be interested in it.

Still, without fail, Gertie double-checked to see we locked the doors. Once she was sure we were safely fastened in, she demanded that we look out the window, take note of what we saw out there, and count our blessings for what we have. "Look, she said. "I want you children to look out the window and see how poor people have to live. Such a shame people have to live like that. I want you to be grateful. Look how they live."

To me, those streets looked like a set at Universal Studios. The broken and boarded-up windows spelled danger and romance.

"Look at that," Gertie said one Sunday, pointing out some clotheslines. "They still hang out their wash."

The buildings on our block all had laundry rooms which really weren't as elegant as Gertie would have us believe. The clotheslines looked friendly. Old shirts waved and flapped as they got reeled in. Moreover, the clotheslines held a hint of the spy business. If you had an accomplice on the other side of the alley, you could send secret messages back and forth, attaching them with a clothespin.

"How dreadful to be poor," Gertie said.

"Low-socioeconomic," Ruth corrected her.

All I knew was I wouldn't have minded being poor, or low-socioeconomic, the way the rest of my family would have minded. Gertie and Herb and Alex talked about those people with pity. Ruth used different terms and talked more about cultural differences and raw deals dealt by society but it boiled down to the same thing. They felt sorry for the kids who hung out on street corners smoking cigarettes and playing radios real loud.

The way I figured it, those kids may have been poor which was, no doubt, a crummy hand, but they saw action. I'd have bet they knew bookies and hookers on a first-name basis. Plus, no one in a neighborhood like that walks alone. Those people stick together. They have gangs. Gangs have jackets and colors. The Warriors. The Jack-Knives. The Jack-Knives' Girls. Everyone, as far as I could see, belonged to a gang. Everyone had friends and backup. "I think this would be a neat place to live," I said.

Alex opened his big mouth and said, "You're so dumb. You have no idea what it would be like to be poor. Think of it, Audrey, if you were poor, you wouldn't have money for your precious movies. How would you like that, Miss Smartypants?"

Alex's lack of imagination was staggering. If I were poor and wanted to go to the movies, surely I would have enough street smarts to figure a way in.

Ruth took her turn to give me a lecture on the disadvantaged and their lack of opportunities. "You," Ruth said, "can be anything you choose."

"What if I choose to be a gangster?" I asked. "Then this would be the perfect training ground, wouldn't it?"

No one paid any more attention to me. "Ignore her when she says things like that," Gertie instructed.

ON ALL sides and from any direction, Aunt Ida was a big, big woman. She was bigger, even, than Fatty Arbuckle. Aunt Ida gave bear hugs to each of my family members, lifting them, one at a time, a good six inches off the ground. When she got to me, Aunt Ida bent all the way down, grabbed my face and squeezed. "You're getting sooo big. The little baby is growing so tall." This was such a big, stupid lie, it embarrassed everyone except Aunt Ida.

Then she herded us over to the dining room table where she brought out a zillion plates, dishes, and platters. "It's all almost burned," Aunt Ida said, "because you were so late. I expected you hours ago." We were, in fact, not late, not even by a minute. This was something we went through every time we came to Aunt Ida's. The way I figured it, it was some sort of game she had going with Gertie.

Not only was the dinner not burned, it practically bordered on raw. There was some ice remaining on the lima beans Aunt Ida spooned into my plate.

"Ida," Gertie said, "I see you use frozen vegetables. I suppose they're very handy. I, of course, wouldn't know. I always use fresh vegetables."

These insults were due to go on all day. It was a well-established pattern with Gertie and Ida.

Aunt Ida sliced off the leg of a boiled chicken and put it next to my icy lima beans. Now, boiled chicken never looks good but this one looked particularly sickly. I stared at it for too long. My stomach did a flip-flop. "May I be excused?" I asked. "I don't feel so well."

To Aunt Ida's way of thinking, if you leave the table without having had at least two helpings of everything, then you must be ready for the hospital. "She's sick," Aunt Ida said. "The baby is sick. You don't take care of her, Gertie. The baby is sick."

"Yeah," I said. "Baby is sick."

Aunt Ida hopped up from the table. Her flesh jiggled at the sudden move. "I'll take you to lie down," she said.

I got up from my seat and let Aunt Ida steer me into her bedroom. Aunt Ida's bedroom smelled old and full of mothballs and Lysol.

"Here." She turned down the bedspread for me. "You take a nappy."

I got under the covers and winced as Aunt Ida planted a wet kiss on my forehead. She stood over me, casting a shadow, while I pretended to sleep. A minute later, she left the room, closing the door behind her.

"She's sleeping comfortably," I heard her tell my family.

The truth was, the minute I'd gotten away from the table, my stomach felt fine. So, I got out of bed and nosed around Aunt Ida's room.

On her dressing table were tubes and jars of goop which, very obviously, didn't have any effect. A hairbrush sat next to some rollers.

None of this stuff held any interest for me. What I was after was on a shelf off to the left of the dressing table. That shelf was where Aunt Ida housed her thimble collection.

These thimbles were the sort you're supposed to use in sewing to keep from pricking your finger. Only, Aunt Ida didn't sew. She didn't use her thimbles for anything except to gather dust. She was a collector, buying a thimble every time she went someplace. They were keepsakes and somewhat fancier than your average thimble.

It was sort of curious that a woman as large as Aunt Ida chose to collect something as small as those thimbles. The way I figured it, she should have been collecting boulders or dinosaur bones.

But Aunt Ida's thimble collection was the pride of her life. She claimed it was a contender for the largest collection in New York. My hunch was that it was the only thimble collection in New York.

That day I studied the thimbles more closely than

when Aunt Ida dragged me in to show them to me. Without her breathing on my neck, I could study each one at my own pace.

Aunt Ida had thimbles from Asbury Park and Atlantic City, New Jersey. There was one from Niagara Falls and another from Bear Mountain. There were thimbles from every attraction in Florida, from Parrot Jungle to Disney World to the Everglades' Glass Bottom Boats. Aunt Ida had a thimble from Maryland and one from Washington D.C., which had a little copper Capitol building glued to the front. Another one was trimmed with blue paint and featured a white horse painted across it. That was the thimble I liked best, from Wild West City. I tried picturing Aunt Ida in Wild West City, wherever that was, but I couldn't get a handle on it.

Although I'd seen the thimble collection many times, I'd never before experienced the urge which came over me as I eyeballed that Wild West City thimble. The urge was to have it. I wanted, for myself, Aunt Ida's Wild West City thimble. And I knew how to get it.

I moved in real close on the shelf and stood on my tiptoes. I knew it was wrong to steal from Aunt Ida, but once you are on the path of crime, there is no turning back. Crimes get bigger and bigger as you go along. There is no room in the criminal world for sentiment. Every movie fan knows that, eventually, criminals steal even from their own mothers. Crime gets in the blood.

I reached up very, very slowly, taking care not to knock anything over. I had to be quiet as a mouse. I was but inches away from the Wild West City thimble, ready to make my grab, when the bedroom door flew open. "Audrey!" It was Aunt Ida.

I spun around. Guilty. Guilty as charged.

"Audrey," Aunt Ida said, "what are you doing out of bed? You should be resting. Oh, you were admiring my pretty thimbles, weren't you?" Aunt Ida was extremely slow on the uptake. Lucky for me.

"Yes, Auntie Ida," I said, making a pouty-lipped, puffy-cheeked, fair impression of Shirley Temple singing "On the Good Ship Lollipop" in *Bright Eyes*.

"My thimbles," she said, "are so beautiful. No one can resist looking at them."

"Very pretty," I said, oozing more innocence.

"Yes, so pretty." Aunt Ida wiped her eye as if the beauty of these thimbles was worth weeping over. "But don't touch, baby. Now, be Auntie Ida's sweetie and get back into bed. We can't have you getting sick on us. You, of all the children, need your rest." Aunt Ida thought I was delicate like Tiny Tim from that Christmas movie about ghosts, the kid who had whooping cough or something. "You need your strength," she said.

Aunt Ida re-tucked me into bed and kissed me again. She smelled of chicken meat.

No sooner did Aunt Ida plop back down at the dinner table, than her sweetie zipped out of bed and pocketed her Wild West City thimble.

■ ■ ■

FOR THE drive home, I pretended to be sick still so I could sit in the front seat. I don't like the back seats of cars. They always seem to be the number two position. I especially didn't like sitting back there with my brother Alex.

When we got upstairs, Gertie insisted the first thing I do was have a bicarbonate of soda.

"I don't want one," I said. "I feel fine. Honest."

"All day you felt sick," Gertie said. "You must have eaten something bad. Ida's food isn't always as fresh as it could be."

The only way to down a bicarbonate of soda successfully is to pretend it is a Tom Collins and you are Dorothy Malone.

Satisfied with my performance, Gertie took the glass and sent me off to bed.

In my hideout, I took the thimble from my pocket and put it on my thumb, the only finger of mine it fit. I wagged it like it was one of those finger puppets Herb used to buy for me when I really was little in all respects.

THE WAY Mr. Eisenstein figured it, the Mae West Festival he held at the Variety was not the success the 3-D Festival had been. "A flop," he said. We sat in the lobby after *Klondike Annie* let out. "No better than any other Saturday."

That wasn't the way I figured it. From my angle, I got three movies for the price of one and didn't get stuck sitting next to Elinore Ditmar in the bargain. Plus, these weren't just any three movies. Mae West was a broad worth knowing. What skills she had. It was a privilege to watch her wrap her leading men around her plump fingers. And those men weren't exactly your average Joes either. Among those who fell for Mae West were the young Cary Grant, Edward Arnold, and even W.C. Fields who was a first-rate con artist in his own right. I learned a number of things from Mae West movies which I planned on putting to good use if I ever got around to looking like a woman.

Mr. Eisenstein finished off the rest of his popcorn and crunched the carton into a ball. "So, tell me," he asked, "what is it you young people want to see? 3-D movies I show. Junk. They flood the gates. I show Mae West. Not such junk and I can't give the tickets away. You're a young person, Audrey. So tell me what young people want to see."

I said a James Cagney Festival would be first-rate. "I could sit through weeks on end of Cagney movies," I said.

"A genius was Cagney," Mr. Eisenstein agreed. "But slowly I'm learning, Audrey. Not too many of us want genius. I run Cagney films very often and almost no one comes. You know that. Yeech," Mr. Eisenstein made a face, "there is no appreciation for the greats. The public wants garbage. It breaks my heart, Audrey, to bring garbage movies into Eisenstein's movie house."

Mr. Eisenstein's next brainstorm turned out to be a Festival of Horror. "What do you think, Audrey?" he asked but didn't wait for me to answer. "I think it's a good idea and an agreeable arrangement," he went on. "I think maybe it will be popular and I don't compromise my ideals. I'll show *Dracula* with Bela Lugosi and *Frankenstein* with Boris Karloff, and *Bride of Frankenstein* I'll throw in for good measure. Those are fine movies but maybe with a little luck, those dummies won't know that. I satisfy Eisenstein and the people. So, All-Day Horror on Saturday. What do you think? A good idea, no?"

A good idea, yes. It was such a good idea that I didn't

go to it. Any enthusiasm I might have had left for the Festival of Horrors was snuffed out by Friday. My entire school was buzzing about the Festival. For two days before, Frank Giordano walked around kissing girls on the neck and saying, "I want to suck your blood." What a twinkie.

WHEN THAT Saturday rolled around, I wasn't too sure what to do with myself. I took Herb's discarded morning newspaper out of the trash. I flipped through it, considering the idea of breaking down and going to a first-run movie, but all that was showing were movies about real-life teenagers with real-life problems. That defeated the purpose of going to the movies in the first place. I went to escape from my problems, not to watch them.

I wandered into the kitchen and found Gertie on her hands and knees. I asked her if she needed some help around the house, figuring at least that would be something to do.

"What's the matter?" Gertie asked. "Are you sick again?"

"No," I said. "I feel fine. I just thought maybe you needed some help."

"I can manage my own house very nicely, thank you!" Gertie acted like I'd insulted her. "Why aren't you outside playing with your friends?"

I shrugged and said I didn't feel like it. "Not in the mood," I said.

Gertie told me not to shrug. She said I'd get permanent neck damage from all that shrugging. "Get, now," she said. "Go on. Go outside and get fresh air and exercise."

I left Gertie in the kitchen attacking the linoleum with a toothbrush. Gertie said that was the only way to get linoleum clean between the cracks.

A FEW WEEKS prior to this aimless Saturday, I'd had a sore throat so Gertie let me stay home from school and watch television. That was when I saw a rerun of *Leave It to Beaver* which came on at ten in the morning. In this episode, Beaver's dorky older brother Wally went away on an overnight camping trip with the Boy Scouts. As Beaver spent most of his life tagging after Wally, he found he had nothing to do that day so he moped around and talked to himself a lot. Finally, he settled in to watch a hole in the street which Con Edison had dug up. There wasn't any action in this hole but pathetic Beaver parked himself on the sidewalk and spent an entire afternoon watching a void.

I was not about to get sucked into spending my Saturday in the same sort of way. I came up with something to do which was to go to the Post Office and have a look at the Wanted posters.

The Wanted posters were tacked to a bulletin board near the main entrance. They were a bit high up for me. I couldn't exactly see eye to eye with the felons, but that wasn't the big loss I'd thought it'd be. The faces on those mug shots looked very much like regular people and nothing like the gangsters in the movies. Nor had any of these criminals pulled any top-notch capers like big jewel heists or cat burglaries, and none of them had fancy monikers either. These petty thieves had average names like Sam Johnson and Richard Stevens. Those are not awesome names, chilling, fear-in-the-guts names like Scarface Al Capone or Legs Diamond or Edward G. Robinson. There was a kid in my Algebra class named Richard Stevens. His nose ran all the time. What kind of name is that for a Wanted poster?

There was one woman on that Post Office bulletin board. Melinda Schwartz was wanted for bombing a building about twelve years ago. She was still on the lam. To me, Melinda Schwartz did not look like anyone's moll. She wasn't wearing a mink coat. No satin dress. No earrings or makeup even. Obviously, Melinda Schwartz never saw Virginia Mayo or else she would have known she was dressed all wrong for the job.

The real thing was such a lousy substitute for the movies. I went home.

The super's mutt was slobbering over a tennis ball when he spotted me coming down the block. His tail beat against the pavement and he yapped at me and then yapped at the ball and then at me.

I picked up the ball, which was wet with dog drool and other kinds of grime. I could just hear Gertie going on about the germs on that ball waiting to ambush me and infect me with a rare tropical disease.

I wouldn't have minded so much coming down with

some exotic illness. I saw that movie about the sickly kid whose one big wish was to meet Babe Ruth. So who shows up at the hospital? None other than William Bendix as the Babe to visit the kid. Then Babe Ruth promised the kid to hit a home run for him in the next game which, of course, he did because the movies are never a disappointment. If I got a rare disease, I would want Pretty Boy Floyd to knock over a bank in my honor.

As I didn't have any plans for the rest of the day, and also because I can be soft on occasion, I killed the better part of an hour tossing that messy tennis ball around for the mutt. The pooch was going mad with excitement. This seemed to be one of the larger events in the dog's life.

When I tired out, he came and sat next to me on the steps. For a minute there, I sort of lost my marbles and forgot he was a dog and not a person. I started running at the mouth about how rotten it felt to be x-ed out of the Variety. "I missed three great movies today," I said, "because of those twinkies from my school. They don't really love the movies. They should leave the theatre free for those of us who know what we're watching."

For a dumb mutt, this dog had a very intelligent mug. He looked like he got my drift.

"So I spent the better part of the day in the Post Office. Someday, there will be a picture of me hanging there. It's possible."

The mutt barked.

"I used to want to be a reporter," I said, "like Lois Lane. Or Citizen Kane who was really Orson Welles. But I think people have to follow their true natures. Answer their calling. And I think mobsterism is in my blood. I feel like I was meant for the life. It's an attraction I feel. . ."

"You're talking to a dog?" My brother Alex, the sneak, had slow-footed it around the building without my spotting him. "You're talking to a dog," he repeated.

I grew hot around the neck and under the collar. "I wasn't talking to the dog, Alex," I said. "I was just thinking out loud and the mutt happened to be here."

Alex said that talking to myself was as much a sign of craziness as talking to a dog and he was going to see to it that I was locked up. "You're not fit to live with society," he said.

It seemed to me that my brother Alex should have been beaten up a lot. If I wasn't so small, I would have had a go at him myself. Well, the way I figured it, he'd be very sorry when I got to be a famous gangster and underworld figure with a mob of my own.

No matter what Alex thought, I wasn't waiting for the mutt to talk back to me or anything. I was just sorting out a few things that were on my mind and the lonely mutt was hanging around. I was being a good egg by not shooing him off was all there was to it. Only Alex made me feel ashamed.

"Go home," I said to the dog. Gangsters have to be very tough. I couldn't let a pair of sad brown eyes get me in the guts. "Get lost," I said, tougher this time. "Scram!" That time the mutt got the message and slunk off with his tail between his legs.

Underworld figures cannot be pushovers. Under any circumstances.

At four o'clock The Million Dollar Movie was showing *Godzilla vs. the Sea Monster*. I'd seen it about a thousand times already. It was nowhere near the quality of monster movie I'd missed that afternoon at the Variety, but it was better than nothing.

Aiming for that movie-theatre feel, I shut off all the lights before plopping into Herb's easy chair. The Million Dollar Movie music, which is Tara's Theme, filled the living room.

Ruth came in and snapped on the overhead light. She was waving some newspaper article she wanted me to read. Generally speaking, Ruth armed with an article to read is worth avoiding. But this article was about a movie museum that had just opened in Queens. I read hungrily.

"Would you like to go there?" Ruth asked.

I squashed the urge to be sarcastic even though Ruth's question was very dumb. Of course I wanted to go.

"How about tomorrow?" Ruth wanted to know.

I guess I must've gone all wide-eyed because Ruth laughed and said, "It's a date, then."

I WAS UP and ready with the sun. Ruth slept somewhat later and dressed at a snail's pace. Eventually, she was ready but wouldn't you know it? We got a broken-down old subway that practically crawled to Queens. It inched from stop to stop and I worried we'd never get there. Then, Ruth insisted we delay even more by having lunch first.

I wolfed down a tuna-fish sandwich in two gulps but Ruth ate very ladylike. Also, she wanted to yak over lunch. She asked one boring question after the next. Questions about school and my long-term plans for life. Periodically, she'd giggle and say, "Isn't this nice? Two sisters out for the day."

Minutes ticked by until I had to say, "Hey, Ruth. You think we could get a move on it? The place could close before you finish eating."

Although I could've gotten in for kid's price, which was half the cost of an adult ticket, Ruth didn't so much as consider the idea. She just slid the money over and said, "Two, please," like there was no question about my age. It was very square of Ruth not to try to save a few bucks at my expense. I hate to say this but Gertie and Herb are not always so square in that area.

The American Museum of the Moving Image was packed with people. Usually, crowds get on my nerves because they tend to push me around but here it was nice. I never knew there were so many of us. Judging from the crowd at the Variety, you'd think movie fans were like dinosaurs. On the way out. But movie fans were here in droves. And they were a snappy looking bunch, I might add. People who could've been movie stars themselves. And I was one of them. I belonged.

The first floor was devoted to movie equipment, projectors, sound machines, stuff like that. In all honesty it didn't thrill me any except for one funny thing. An old TV set on display was the exact same one my Aunt Ida had in her livingroom. Even Ruth got a kick out of that and said, "Imagine. Aunt Ida's got a museum-quality television."

Upstairs was where my heart raced. In a panic that I wouldn't get to see it all, I spun around in little circles not knowing where to look first.

"Let's start from here," Ruth said, "and follow straight along. That way, we'll be sure to see everything."

Ruth's plan started us at a series of photographs of Greta Garbo. Studying each picture, she asked, "Who is this, Audrey?"

For a person with a lot of education, Ruth could be very ignorant. "It's Garbo," I told her. "Greta Garbo."

"Oh," Ruth said. "So, that's her. She was very beautiful, wasn't she?"

"Is," I corrected Ruth. "She is beautiful. Movie greats never leave us," I explained. "She's still here. On film."

At the screens with telephone hookups, Ruth got a little impatient with me. See, there were ten screens with telephones attached. Each screen was showing a different movie. I'd expected to pick up the phone and hear the movie. But surprise! What I got on the line was the directors chatting away telling stories about the stars of the movies. And tales of the old studio days in

Hollywood. Talking to me on the phone like they were old friends of mine.

"Come on, Audrey. There's lots more to see," Ruth said for the third time.

Only I couldn't tear myself away. Aside from being very interested in what they were saying, it had been a long, long time since anyone had spoken to me on the phone. Of course, I knew this was a recording. It wasn't like we were really having a regular conversation where I could talk back. But it was close.

"Audrey," Ruth said again. "Let's go. You don't want to spend the whole day on one thing."

As much as I hated to hang up, Ruth was right.

While she was cooing silly over a Disney exhibit, I wandered off to the photographs and models of the old movie theatres. The sort Mr. Eisenstein had told me about. Palaces. In a glass case was a dollhouse-sized Roxy Theatre. My ex-friend Rosalie used to have a fancy dollhouse, but next to this, Rosalie's dollhouse looked to be from Skid Row. The little Roxy Theatre had gold ceilings and gold staircases and box seats which were private balconies for two. I tried to imagine what it must've been like to see a movie in such a place. It had to have been a movie within a movie.

"What's that?" Ruth joined me at the Roxy. "An opera house?"

"No, it's a movie theatre," I told her proudly.

Ruth wanted me to check out a gizmo that produced special effects but I explained to her why I didn't want to. "There are some things I don't want to know," I said. "Sometimes, it's best to leave the mystery alone."

Much to Ruth's credit, she understood that.

Without even planning it, we'd saved the best for last, like chocolate cake after a great dinner. We came to The Magic Mirror. A skinny man was there ahead of us and, right before our eyes, there was the skinny man's head perched on John Wayne's body.

I let Ruth go ahead of me because I was too excited. I needed to catch my breath.

"Ready?" the man at the control panel asked Ruth.

"Yes," Ruth tucked some loose hairs behind her ears.

The man pressed a button and there she stood wearing Scarlett O'Hara's gown. My sister looked beautiful —only, to my humiliation, she didn't know who she was. "Is this from a Western?" she asked.

"Oh, fiddle-dee-dee," the man said. "That's Miss Scarlett's dress."

"From *Gone With the Wind*, Ruth," I said.

It was my turn. As if the guy at the controls could read dreams, I got Marilyn Monroe. My mug on Marilyn Monroe's body. It was that famous shot of her in the white dress swirling above her knees: all legs and chest. I looked sensational with long legs and hips and bosoms in living technicolor.

I could've stayed at The Magic Mirror forever but there was a whole slew of movie fans waiting to see themselves as their favorite stars. Because they were fans, and not some average pack of twinkies, I didn't want to hold up their dreams any longer.

This museum also had real movie theatres where you could just walk in and watch a movie beginning to end, but Ruth said we didn't have time for that. She said it like she was really sorry, which she didn't have to be. I'd seen so many wonderful things, I didn't think my memory could hold on for more.

The instant we boarded the subway for home, the day caught up to me. I got really tired and leaned against Ruth. My sister put her arm around me.

"Did you have a good time?" she asked.

"Mmmmmm," I said, my eyes shutting.

"You know, Audrey," Ruth's voice got sugary and gooey. "We all love you very much. You do know that, don't you?"

I don't remember if I answered Ruth or not because at that moment I fell asleep. Conked right out like a little kid after a big day.

The next thing I knew, Ruth was shaking me and saying, "Wake up, Audrey. We're home."

I sat up and felt exactly like Dorothy did after having been to Oz. There is something over the rainbow and I'd been there.

IT WAS on Tuesday that I saw *If I Had a Million*, which was like eight episodes of that old TV show *The Millionaire*. Each person in the stories gets a cool million bucks. A million bucks can change a person's life for the better. It was a nice movie which let you feel like good things can happen at a moment's notice.

The next day, which had to be a Wednesday, I came out of my building on my way to school and found a mob scene on the street. It appeared as if each and every one of my neighbors had filed out and filled the block. My street was a sea of people of all sizes and shapes.

Standing on the points of my black Keds, I craned my neck to see over the mass of ladies and kids and some fathers on their way to work. Gertie hated those Keds of mine. She said they were bad for my feet and would cripple me. Also, according to Gertie, they looked cheap. Gertie and I had been waging an ongoing battle over what I wore. I had taken to wearing a lot of black. As every movie fan knows, black is the color of the underworld. Gertie said I looked like I was on my way to a funeral. This made sense because the underworld has to be ready for any turn of events. Underworld figures never know when a friend will meet up with the wrong end of a Saturday Night Special.

All I could see was the neighborhood ladies pulling their cardigans over their bosoms and men shaking their heads. I tried to make my way through the crowd to the center but no one would give an inch. Everyone was after a front row seat.

I spied Mrs. Korngold ahead of me and wormed my way over to her by crawling between people's legs. Mrs. Korngold had to know what was going on. If she ever redirected her snooping, Mrs. Korngold would have made an ace sleuth.

"Mrs. Korngold," I tugged at her elbow. "What happened?"

"Oh, little one," Mrs. Korngold said. "You shouldn't look. Such a little one should not see such a thing." Despite what she'd just said, Mrs. Korngold had every intention of letting me look. She did a neat little side-step allowing me to slide into her spot.

It was the dog. The super's mutt. He was all busted up on the pavement. "He went off the roof," Jennifer Wallach said. Jennifer Wallach was a year younger than me but a good six inches taller. "The dog just went off the roof," she repeated.

■ ■ ■

I TRIED wiping the picture of the mutt all broken up out of my mind. Only I couldn't seem to do it. Like reel-to-reel, it played over and over again in my head. Shutting my eyes only made the picture clearer.

My first class of the day was history. I took a seat in the back row. I wanted to blend in with the wall. I wanted to be left alone.

As a rule, Mr. Neville, my history teacher, and I got along. We had a common bond which we found out about when we began studying Abraham Lincoln. Luck was with me because just two days before I'd seen a double feature, Henry Fonda in *Young Mr. Lincoln* and Humphrey Bogart in *The Caine Mutiny*. I had about a thousand facts right at my fingertips which I listed off rapid fire. I thought I was the class hot shot but then I got so carried away, I got mixed up and said, "So Mr. Lincoln rolled these little metal balls around in his hand." Only that was Humphrey Bogart as the crazy sea captain in *The Caine Mutiny*.

Mr. Neville got on to me. "I gather you've seen the film *Young Mr. Lincoln*," he said. He asked me if it was primarily historical films I was interested in.

"Sure," I said. "Those too. I like all movies. Especially if they're old."

That's when Mr. Neville owned up to being a movie fan himself. Except he called it "a film buff." Sometimes, after class we'd yak about the movies. Often he suggested I see some foreign films. Mr. Eisenstein didn't show those at the Variety. He said there wasn't even enough time to show all the great American ones.

Anyway, Mr. Neville liked me even though I wasn't any whiz at history. I didn't fail but I wasn't so good with dates. The only way I could recall a date is to remember which movie I saw on such and such a day. Like I could remember seven Tuesdays ago because that's when I saw *The Oklahoma Kid*. You don't forget a movie starring Bogart and Cagney. But dates in history don't have movies attached. The only way I could have possibly remembered dates in history was to study them.

I put my head down on the desk like I was sick and closed my eyes. Real hard I tried to picture something nice like Gene Kelly tap dancing.

"Audrey?" I heard Mr. Neville say. "Would you please answer the question?"

"What question?" I asked.

"I asked for the nations involved with the War of 1812."

"What difference does it make?" I wanted to know. "All the people are dead now. They died in the war or they died of diseases or they died because no one cared. So what difference does it make now?" For a reason which I didn't understand, this was making me angry. I got keyed up and I demanded an answer. "Tell me," I sort of shouted. "Tell me in a way that makes sense."

Mr. Neville didn't have any light to shed. All he had was the usual history teacher type of twaddle about history repeating itself and learning by our mistakes.

110

"There are no second shots at life," I said. "It doesn't matter in the end, does it?"

Mr. Neville turned away from me and called on that twinkie Sharon Kessler. She lapped up the opportunity to be Goody Two Shoes.

"Very good, Sharon," Mr. Neville said. "Perhaps Audrey can take a lesson from you."

To that I said, "No thanks. I like my nose the color it is."

The fact that Mr. Neville was obviously annoyed might have bothered me on any other day but not that one. That was the day my blood began to run cold. I didn't want anyone to like me ever again.

It was clear to me I was in no shape to go to the Bat-Lady's class so I ducked into the bathroom and locked myself in a stall. I put the lid of the toilet down and sat, drawing up my legs and tucking my knees under my chin.

I felt safe, all curled up in the cold, clammy bathroom. When I heard the bathroom door swing and the clickety-click of high heels on tile, I pulled myself in tighter until I resembled a basketball. I would have been as concealed as the Purple Gang hiding out in the Badlands except I sneezed. A muffled a-choo.

"Who is that?" a too-too familiar voice asked. It reminded me of nothing less than ten fingernails scraping across the blackboard.

I kept still. The code-word was "mum." I played it cool, hoping the Bat-Lady would think it was her imagination playing tricks on her. Apparently though, the Bat-Lady had seen the same TV shows I'd seen. She climbed up on the toilet in the neighboring stall and peered over the top at me. "Audrey," she snapped. "Why aren't you in class?"

"I'm sick," I said, moaning and rocking on my perch for effect.

"You are not sick. You're cutting class. Come out of there this instant."

Defeated, but only for the moment, I got up and slid open the lock. The door swung back for me to greet my captor.

"To the principal's office with you, young lady."

The Bat-Lady marched me out of the bathroom double time. "Go on," she said. "Get to the principal's office and tell him what you've done. Tell him you've cut class." The Bat-Lady may have known a few old TV tricks but she hadn't kept up with the workings of a devious mind. At the turn-off in the corridor, she went back to the classroom and I went directly to my locker, got my jacket and exited out the fire door. I ran.

I ran as if I were being chased, as if I were running through alleyways and scaling chain-link fences and racing across rooftops. I ran like it was nighttime and the law was at my heels, like I was hearing sirens closing in on me from all directions. I ran to the safe-house, to the Variety.

The Miracle Woman was playing. It starred Barbara Stanwyck, although for the life of me I couldn't say what it was about even though I sat through it two and a half times. I wasn't able to focus.

When I got to my block, I stood at the corner. I was surprised to find it empty. I guess I thought I'd find it as I left it, all those people gaping at the dead pooch. Only, the street was deserted except for a handful of little girls playing hopscotch. Hopscotch dies hard in Canarsie. As a sport, we take hopscotch seriously. The season lasts until the first snowfall.

Those little girls weren't having a first-rate game. It wasn't in the competition level league but I stood around and watched the squirts anyway. Due to the fact that mothers in Canarsie have a mortal fear of the cold, these kids were hopping around like robots with limited movement due to the layers of sweaters and jackets and leg warmers they had on. Twelvesies was proving especially difficult for them.

"Hey Audrey," one of the kids called, "you want to play?"

"Scram, kid," I said. "I'm nothing but trouble."

The kid giggled which wasn't supposed to happen so I moved on down the street until I got to the spot where the mutt had offed himself. I looked for the chalk outline where the body had been. In the movies, there is always a chalk outline to take the place of the corpse. But this time there wasn't anything. There ought to have been some sort of marker. Even if a chalk outline would have gotten washed away eventually in the rain or snow, it would have been better than nothing. It wouldn't have been like it never happened.

I stood in front of the building and looked up, shielding my eyes from the sun. The sun in Canarsie is very bright right before it sets. That's because Canarsie is near the water and the sun reflects off the oil slicks.

I felt heavy breathing down my neck which turned

out not to be Melvin Purvis but, rather, Leo Shumsky. Melvin Purvis was the G-man who caught John Dillinger, shot him cold. Leo Shumsky lived on my block and was also in my homeroom. Leo was the record-breaking twinkie. He had asthma and thighs that rubbed away the corduroy of his pants.

"I saw it," Leo said to me. "I saw the dog fall. I was on my way to school and I looked up in time. He just went off. Like this." Leo stuck his arms straight out like Superman and made a whistling noise. I couldn't tell if that was supposed to be the sound of the dog falling or if it was Leo's asthma kicking up. "You didn't see him fall," he said. "But I did. I saw the whole thing."

"Be quiet, Leo," I said, "or you might have an accident, too." He was such a twinkie that he allowed himself to be bullied by the likes of me. I was about a quarter his size. Leo must have known that many great gangsters, both on the screen and off, were small of stature. That didn't make us any less menacing.

I left Leo quaking in his boots, and even though I wasn't exactly in any hurry to get there, I went home.

Now, Gertie had 20/20 hearing. No matter how quietly I opened the door and where she was in the apartment, Gertie heard the turn of the knob. "Audrey?" she called out. "Is that you? Come here a minute. In the kitchen."

"In the kitchen" meant that Gertie was busy cooking and couldn't leave the stove. I pretended I didn't hear her. I had a nagging suspicion that I could be in hot water. Chances were excellent that this time around, the Bat-Lady had taken the drastic measure of telephoning Gertie and ratting on me. I went directly to my room, hoping to delay any confrontation long enough to come up with a reasonable lie with which to cover my act.

Without permission, Gertie opened my bedroom door and came in. "I got a phone call today, Audrey," she said. I felt my stomach sink. "From that lovely Mrs. Margolis," Gertie added.

"Who?" I asked.

"Your English teacher," Gertie said.

"Oh, you must mean the Bat-Lady. You confused me with the word lovely."

Gertie instructed me not to be so fresh and then filled me in on the nature of the call. "Audrey, Mrs. Margolis said you cut her class today and then when she sent you to the principal's office, you left school altogether."

"Is that all she said?" I asked, wondering how many lies I'd have to come up with in a flash.

"Yes," Gertie said. "But Audrey, this is serious." Apparently in her current rage, the Bat-Lady neglected to mention the other run-ins she and I had had. Gertie thought this was my first offense. First offenders always have it easier.

However, first offense or not, cutting school, according to Gertie, was serious business, practically a felony. "Do you want to tell me why you cut school?"

If she'd given me five more minutes, surely I could

have come up with some sort of an answer but in this time frame, all I could do was shrug.

"You saw," Gertie said. "The dog? This morning. You saw?"

I shrugged again.

"Stop with the shrugging," Gertie said. "You'll hurt your neck and become paralyzed with all that shrugging. So, you got upset over the dog and didn't go to school? Is that it?" Gertie had invented a lie for me, which was much appreciated because I just wasn't up to inventing one myself. "These things happen," she went on. "Try not to take it too hard."

"I'll try," I said. For special effect, I worked up a tear or two. To my surprise, that bit of sniveling came easier than I thought it would. As a rule, tough cookies don't cry.

Gertie and I had dinner alone that night. Herb had to work late, Ruth was attending a lecture, and Alex was on the road with the debating team. The apartment seemed to be very quiet even though Gertie kept up a running monologue all during the meal. She talked about soap powders and the price of broccoli and a lot of other things I didn't hear because I wasn't listening.

During dessert, Gertie reached into her apron pocket and took out a five-dollar bill. "Here," she said. "Tomorrow after school why don't you go shopping and buy yourself something. I find shopping lifts my spirits when I feel a little down."

I never imagined Gertie felt down. Or up. Or sideways. Gertie was my mother. She was supposed to be a constant.

116

"Maybe," she said, "you could go with one of your girlfriends from school." Gertie sounded so hopeful when she said that. There were times I thought it bothered her more than it bothered me that I didn't have any friends. Just to ease her mind, I used to lie to her sometimes and tell her I was out with Cassandra or Melody or Imogene. Gertie seemed to know, however, that these were lies for her benefit. In such instances, she didn't ask her usual zillion and a half questions; questions like what does Cassandra's father do for a living? Or how are Imogene's grades at school? Normally, Gertie had her nose in everywhere but when I'd lie about friends, she let it drop.

"You ought to make some nice new girlfriends," Gertie said not for the first time. "Sometimes, I think maybe you're not as nice to the girls in your class as you could be. You have to make an effort to make friends, Audrey. You can't sit around waiting for them to call you. You have to start the ball rolling. I think you would be pleasantly surprised if you called up one of the nice girls in your class and asked her to go out with you some afternoon."

I stared into my chocolate pudding so I wouldn't have to look my mother in the face. I just wasn't in the mood to hear any more of the pep talk about how some little girl is sitting at home right this minute wishing I would call her up.

For perhaps the first time in her life, Gertie got the message. She rose and cleared the table. "I suppose it would be okay," she said, "if you wanted to watch a little television." Whenever Gertie felt sorry for me, she lightened up on the TV restrictions. I had her in the palm of my hand.

I turned on the eight o'clock movie which turned out not to be a movie but two re-runs of *Columbo* episodes back to back. I kept seeing flashes, like edited splices, of dogs where bodies were supposed to be and every now and then, Peter Falk appeared to be my mother. I must have been very, very tired.

THE DAY after the mutt did the deep six, *It Should Happen to You* was showing at the Variety. It's about Gladys Glover who is a sweet sort of nobody until she rents out a Times Square billboard and puts her name up in lights. Then she becomes famous and finds love in the bargain. When a movie like that is over, you feel hopeful, you believe you've got a chance. That is the reason I didn't want to go to it. If Gladys Glover got shot at the end or ended up getting evicted from her apartment, I would have gone to see it, but I was still feeling a bit raw. A nice movie like *It Should Happen to You* just wasn't on my menu for that day. I had other business to attend to.

I boarded the King's Highway bus. Destination: King's Plaza Mall. I avoided face to face contact with the bus driver in case he was questioned by the police later on. I didn't want to chance his remembering me

119

although that wasn't likely. The bus was filled like a sardine can. There was standing room for me only because of my size.

At the mall, me and about a thousand ladies got off the bus. I went directly to Latson's. That was Gertie's favorite store. She took me shopping there for new outfits. Consequently, I was familiar with the layout.

It had to be a department store because there are so many people in them. In department stores there is never a sales lady hovering over you unless you look like a big spender. That was not something I had to worry about. In a department store, I could go about doing what I'd come to do without attracting attention. It would be assumed I was nothing more than a squirt of a kid here with my mother who was most likely in the dressing room. I had a ready-made cover.

First, I cased the joint. Sizing up Housewares, Shoes, and Pocketbooks, I wandered into the evening gown department where I found the gown of my future. It was a real dark-blue affair. Like midnight with a plunging neckline. Around the hem, purple sequins sparkled like rain on the pavement. It was a knockout of a dress. Someday, I thought, that sweet number would be mine.

Just for the fun of it, I checked out Lingerie, scouting for the sort of finery I'd wear under my evening gown. When the time came. My instincts, along with the picture of Carroll Baker in *Baby Doll*, told me satin was the way to go. The one for me was hanging on display. It was peach colored and creamy. I reached out to touch it when a sales lady stepped between me and the rack. "What are you doing here, little girl?" she asked.

"Just browsing," I told her.

"Well, this is no place for you. Now run along." That hurt more than she could ever have imagined, and I might have said a few insulting things in return except I caught sight of myself in a full-length mirror. My crew-neck sweater showed no hints of promise. Besides, I had things to do.

I'd once read a newspaper account of a woman who made off with a television set between her legs. While concealing a TV under your dress is possible, I also knew better than to try something so advanced. My plan of action was to palm a small item of great worth and make it disappear.

This limited me to the cosmetics counter or jewelry. A tube of lipstick, I was confident, could be made to vanish quicker than a wink—but cosmetics seemed rinky-dink. A jewel heist, on the other hand, sounded like music to my ears.

Latson's had two jewelry counters: the real stuff and the fakes. Even though I was set on clipping something real, criminals must survey and weigh the situation carefully. The good gold and diamonds were kept behind locked glass cases. Sales ladies acted like watchdogs over those goods. They wore keys on cords around their necks. That was discouraging.

I moseyed on over to the fakes. Right off, I noticed the clerks yakking with each other. They didn't look at me twice. Should they be questioned later, after the manager discovered the loss, they wouldn't remember a thing. Even under hypnosis, they wouldn't have recalled my face. I pictured the interrogation. "I didn't see anyone, detective. Did you see anyone, Martha? No, Martha didn't see anyone."

The fakes counter was littered with plastic pearls and lime-green beads and bracelets made from papier-maché but some of the fakes, I noted, were pretty good. It wasn't all junk. There were some rhinestones which could have been diamonds and some silver earrings which looked like sterling silver to me. I might have gone for a rhinestone pin except I zeroed in on this little box for keeping pills in. You could have kept coins in it too. It was the size of a silver dollar and the lid was mosaic. Genuine mosaic. Not like our kitchen floor linoleum which was meant to look like real mosaic but wasn't. The lid on this box was set by hand, probably by monks in Italy. I'd heard they did stuff like that for a living. Actually, there was a very good chance that this wasn't fake at all. It might have been the real thing but, by human error, had ended up at the costume jewelry counter.

I thought about Harry Houdini in the movies, played by Tony Curtis. Among other spectacular things, Harry Houdini made objects vanish into thin air as easily as he breathed. I thought about that hard as I picked up the little box and made a fist around it, jammed it into my jacket pocket, loosened my grip, and eased the merchandise from my hand. I came up clean. It was that simple.

I stood fixed in my spot, basking in the glow of victory, when I caught some woman looking at me. Not a sales lady, but a regular person who must have been a customer. For a split second, I felt a hint of panic. Could she have seen me? My hands were just about to sweat when she smiled at me. I smiled broadly for her. The coast was clear.

With no further dawdling, I went to the nearest exit, pausing only to read the sign posted on the door. It said: Shoplifters Will Be Prosecuted to the Fullest Extent of the Law.

"You've got to catch me first, wise guy," I said.

I stood at the bus stop thinking about my first professional job, now completed. It was clean. No snags. No mix-ups. I'd committed a perfect crime. When they made the movie of my life, this might make for a good opening scene, the afterglow of my first real heist.

By the time I got home I was so pleased with myself, I'd nearly forgotten all about the super's mutt being no longer among the living. Actually, I remembered in a sort of pathetic way. I remembered once I was already on the lookout for him, prepared to let him sniff the mosaic box while I recounted the details of my perfect heist. Remembering nearly burst my bubble.

So, I gave myself a talking-to about not being a softie. There is no room for sentimentalities in the underworld, of which I was now a part. "Hey," I said to no one in particular, "the mutt couldn't take the heat."

I STRETCHED out on the bed and felt in my pocket for the pillbox. I ran my fingers over the mosaic like I was reading Braille and it had a story to tell. I knew all about how Braille operated because I'd seen *The Miracle Worker*. The version I'd seen featured Anne Bancroft as the teacher and Patty Duke as Helen Keller. There was another version of that story floating around, a made-for-TV version where Patty Duke, having grown up, played the teacher. I missed that one, even though Gertie went so far as to suggest I watch it, because *Ocean's Eleven* was on a different station at the same time. That was no contest. Not with Frank Sinatra, Peter Lawford, Dean Martin, and Sammy Davis, Jr., pulling a Las Vegas holdup.

Satisfied that I could identify the pattern of the mosaic by touch alone, I took the box from my pocket to have another gander at it. It was a beaut. That box, with its itsy red and blue and green and black tile lid, was the sweetest thing I owned, not at all the same as the chalk I'd borrowed or a hat lifted by mistake. Stealing an item as fine as this is not in the same ball park even as making off with a candy bar. If you clip a Snickers, you eat the evidence and that's the end of that. This box was the sort of candy I could have gone to the slammer for. Stealing this sort of item had to be a Class-A felony. I could have gotten years.

Eventually, I knew, I'd have to find a fence. In the movies, the crooks always know fences. Often, the fence was a guy named Johnny, seen only in the shadows. Other times, it was the pawnbroker who everyone is on to. One thing I did know, fences weren't listed in the Yellow Pages. I would have to do some asking around, have a talk with one of the boys. I would do this as soon as I found out who "the boys" were.

I heard Ruth come home and Gertie waylay her in the kitchen. I listened to them discuss me. Whispering was not an art my family was skilled at.

Gertie was telling Ruth that I was still behaving oddly. That's what she said. "I'm sure it's the dog," Gertie said. "What else could it be? She saw it dead on the ground. Yesterday, she ran away from school and today, she comes in without so much as hello and goes straight to bed."

Ruth began to quote chapter and verse from her dopey psychology textbooks. "She needs to confront this," Ruth said. "She has to talk it out. We mustn't allow her to keep feelings of grief bottled up. It's not healthy," Ruth said.

"Bad for the stomach," Gertie echoed.

Ruth came into my bedroom toting along her let's-be-pals routine. Ruth could be very patronizing at times. "So kiddo . . ." she sat on the edge of my bed. "How's it going?"

"Okey-dokey." Sarcasm sailed way over Ruth's head, hit the ceiling and got lost.

"So, tell me," Ruth moved in closer, "what's been going on in that noodle of yours?" I swear, that's exactly how she said it. What's been going on in that noodle of yours. I nearly choked.

"Nothing," I said. "It's running on empty."

Ruth said she didn't think that was so. "I think," she said, "there is something you'd like to talk about."

"You mean death," I said.

"Well, yes." Ruth thought this was a breakthrough. I pictured her going to Hunter College the next day and telling her class about this. "Would you like to talk about death?" she asked.

"No," I said.

This stymied my sister but not for long. Lighting up with another scheme, she put her arm around me in that big sisterly way and said, "What do you say we do something together on Saturday? We could go ice skating. Or," she came up with a better idea, "we could go back to the Museum of the Moving Image. Would you like that?"

A return trip to the museum was tempting. Very tempting. But I had other plans for Saturday. "No can do, Ruth," I said. "*Dark Passage* is playing at the Variety. It's on the top of my must-see list."

126

Ruth wanted to know if she could go to the movie with me. I'd made that mistake once before. She hounded me all through it. "Who is that man?" and "Why is he lurking in the backround like that?" Ruth asked about two zillion dumb questions which would've been answered if she'd have just shut up and watched the screen. I wasn't about to go through that again. Especially not with a Bogart-Bacall movie. No dice. "Not a good idea," I said.

Ruth actually had the nerve to ask me to skip the movie. "Come on," she said, "just this once, Audrey. After all, it's only a film."

That's how little Ruth knew about movies. Anyone who could call *Dark Passage* "only a film" doesn't have a clue as to what it means to be a movie fan.

I explained to her that missing a "must see" was not in the realm of possibility.

"So," Ruth said, "then what about after the movie? If you go to a noon showing, I could pick you up at two and we could go out for an ice cream."

Whoop-dee-do. An ice cream. Almost-notorious crime figures do not go out for ice cream with their big sisters. Anyway, I had another job planned for after the movie. "I have to go to the store then," I said.

She didn't give up easily. Ruth thought it would be great fun if we went to the store together. "We'll go shopping together like two sisters. Because we are sisters." Ruth said that as if she were first making this discovery.

"I won't be doing any shopping at the store," I said.

Ruth never learned that there are some questions best off not asked. "Why then," she asked, "are you going to the store if not to shop? Are you going to meet a boy, Audrey?" She thought she was on to something. "Come on, you can tell me."

I let a long pause settle between us and then I said, "I'm going to rob the joint."

I dropped honesty in Ruth's lap and she acted like it was a hot potato. She had no idea what to do with it. "You're upset about the dog, aren't you?" That was one of the hazards of being a psychology major. Ruth believed everything was double-talk.

"Just leave the dead dog out of this," I said. "Just leave the dead dog out of everything. Just understand I don't care about the dog. I hated that dog anyway. Leave me alone."

Ruth was dense. First she wouldn't buy that I really was going to the store to steal. Then she wouldn't accept that I indeed wished her to take a walk. "Blow, Ruth," I said. "Vamooose. Scram."

"Audrey . . ." Ruth smoothed the hair on top of my head, ". . . I really think you need to talk this one out. It's obviously been traumatic for you. Come on. Talk to me."

"I'm no canary," I said. "I'm not singing. I'm no egg to be cracked. Got that?"

"Please, Audrey. You really need to talk." Ruth went on at length about how in times of need people don't always get off their chests what's on their minds. "But," she said, "they give out signals that they need to."

I gave Ruth a signal. I pulled the bedspread up over

128

my head. I was like a statue before they pull the sheet off it.

Ruth asked me to come out from under. "You can't run away from your feelings," she said. "You can't hide, Audrey. Not for long."

Maybe I couldn't have stayed there forever but I did manage to stay still long enough for Ruth to tire of talking to a lump. Her parting words were, "If you change your mind I'll be happy to listen to you."

Ruth may have said that but I knew it wasn't so. She might have been willing to sit and hear me out and ask what she believed were probing questions, but Ruth wouldn't have really listened. No one really listened.

When I heard Ruth's voice coming from the kitchen saying, "I can't get through to her," I came out from under wraps. Taking the pillbox with me, I went to the bathroom. I locked the bathroom door and moved the laundry hamper, fixing it under the doorknob for double security.

I wanted to check myself out in the mirror. I was looking for signs that I'd changed. There should have been a sign to indicate I was in the life now. I'd entered a profession which should have brought some hard lines around my mouth. Or at least a scar running from my left eye down my cheek. I expected to look much tougher. Older. I expected to have the sort of face which would make people, nice folks, not want to mess with me. Only the mirror wasn't in agreement. I looked like me. I looked like Audrey. I looked like every other kid who was fourteen but appeared to be ten.

My face was still round and pudgy cheeked. My eyes

weren't at all hardened, and my seven freckles (two on each cheek, one on my chin and two on my nose) were still there.

I decided my expression needed working on. I creased my forehead, which made my eyes slit like I was looking past a haze of cigarette smoke. That wasn't bad but I found I couldn't hold it for long. I tried on a sneer but that ended as a tic so I made my lips go pouty instead. When Carolyn Jones was Mickey Rooney's moll in *Baby Face Nelson* she wore a pout through the whole movie. It worked very well for Carolyn Jones but it reduced me to looking like a six-year old who was about to cry. That wasn't desirable. I was working up a look of contempt when Gertie came rapping at the bathroom door. "Audrey," she called as if I were on the other side of a mountain. "Audrey, what are you doing? Come out of there."

I did a Cagney impression for my mother. "I'm not coming out alive."

"You sound sick," Gertie said. "Are you sick in there?"

I switched over to Greta Garbo and told Gertie, "I vant to be alone."

I had about as much of a chance of being alone as I did rolling lucky sevens all night. Gertie was tugging so hard at the bathroom door, I thought she'd pull it clean from the hinges. "Please, Audrey. I'm begging you to come out of there. It's not healthy to lock yourself in the bathroom. Audrey, please. It was only a dog. It's not like it was a person. It was only a dog."

130

I put the laundry hamper back against the wall and unlocked the door. With my hands in my pockets, one of them wrapped around the mosaic box, I brushed by my mother. The concealed stolen goods passed under her nose. That was a little thrill all my own.

In the living room, I snapped on the television. A detective show, the one which starred James Garner, was on reruns. I was crazy about James Garner. I sat in Herb's easy chair.

Just as James Garner was about to nail the criminal, my brother Alex came home. "I see you're rotting your mind with all that TV garbage again," Alex said to me, but I wasn't listening.

Alex was not worthy of my attention so I didn't give him any. I kept my eye on James Garner. In this series, he was a jailbird himself before he got a governor's parden and became a private investigator. That was one of the reasons he was so cool. He wasn't entirely straight.

Getting ignored drove Alex insane. He thought he was so important. He would stop at nothing and stoop lower than the sidewalk to get attention. Alex believed the way to get me to take notice was to dig at me. "So," he said, "I heard your friend, the super's dog, got killed yesterday."

Alex, being the twinkie he was, once again was a day late with the news. Little did he realize that by now I was a hardened criminal. Hardened criminals are very used to having their friends bite the bullet. Maybe yesterday Alex would have managed to upset me with that poke at my sensitivities, but yesterday Alex was busy at his meeting of the Royal Order of Twinkies and so he missed his opportunity.

"Old scoop," I said.

"Stupid dog didn't even know he was at the edge," Alex said, only I was back to pretending Alex didn't exist. "Only a dog that hung around with you could have been that stupid."

From her spot in the kitchen, Gertie called out to Alex. He jumped right into form and obediently went to her.

"Alex," I heard Gertie say, "be nice to your sister. She's a little upset today."

Rather than have to be nice to his sister, Alex went to his room where he stayed, probably getting hot over his stamp collection, until Herb came home. In our house, that was the equivalent of the dinner bell.

Gertie dished out dinner and started up a conversation with herself which had to do with how the price of vegetables was going through the roof. "That's seventy-nine cents worth of string beans growing cold on your plate, Audrey," she said. Whenever she talked about vegetables, I got this picture of them piled in stacks like poker chips. Brussels sprouts were red chips, lima beans could've been blue chips, and white chips were asparagus. Somewhere, there ought to have been a window with a skinny man in a vest and suspenders behind it where I could've cashed in my vegetables for money.

With my string beans I made crisscrosses to look like

bars to a jail cell. My mother told me to quit playing with my food and poured me a glass of milk.

I used to refuse to drink milk on the grounds that it was a beverage for children until I saw *Guys and Dolls*. Big Jule from Chicago, who was indeed a tough character, ordered milk throughout the movie. He ordered milk with one of the toughest accents in all of moviedom. The way I figured it, if Big Jule from Chicago could drink milk, so could Little Audrey from Canarsie.

I was busy breaking out of my string-bean prison when Alex said, "I wouldn't have much of an appetite if I were Audrey, considering her behavior at school." Alex thought he was bringing news by announcing how I'd skipped out the day before. Little did the twinkie know that Gertie had already pardoned me for it.

"I didn't do anything wrong," I said.

"Oh," replied Alex, "on top of your other crimes you're a liar too."

"What crimes?" Herb came to life but only briefly.

"Yeah Alex," I said. "What crimes? You don't know nothing about no crimes."

Alex corrected my grammar. I should've known better than to waste a good movie line on him. "You could be sitting at the same table with a real criminal," I challenged him, "and you wouldn't even know it."

"What's with this talk of criminals?" Gertie wanted to know. "This is not a subject for the dinner table. Now, let's talk nice before we ruin our stomach linings. And you, Audrey, eat your dinner."

"I do not want my dinner." I pushed my plate away

with a little too much muscle behind it. It crashed into Ruth's water glass, upsetting it. Her string beans went for a swim.

"Audrey, please. It was only a dog," Gertie said.

I got up from my chair, knocking that over, too, in the process. "How many times do I have to tell you? I don't care about the lousy mutt."

In the living room, I switched on the TV. Over a commercial for corn flakes I heard Gertie say, "She's upset about the dog."

THE WEATHER turned for the worse; cold and rainy. I couldn't go out for lunch any more and I had to eat in the cafeteria. From the movies, I knew there was a certain type of criminal who walked alone; the antisocial ones. I decided to use that sort as my role model. I gave a thumbs down to the loser's table and found an empty one in the back next to the teacher's dining room. I took a seat there and called it home.

On Monday, one of the losers, a mouse of a boy called Alvin, came over to my table and put his hand on the seat next to mine. "Is this seat taken?" he asked.

"Yeah," I said. "It's taken. Get lost."

After school, I saw *Marked Woman*. That's the movie where Bette Davis turns state's evidence against the Lucky Luciano character. Not even Bette Davis was to be trusted. Rats are everywhere. Criminals have morals, too, and ratting is a no-no. But it goes to show you, you can't trust anyone. The sunny side to that street was that I didn't have anyone to trust anyhow.

When *Marked Woman* was over, Mr. Eisenstein invited me to join him for a soda. Discussion of the movie led to talk about the big cheese criminals of Mr. Eisenstein's day. His day meant when he was around my age. He remembered Lucky Luciano but he didn't remember Bette Davis ratting on him until he saw the movie. Mr. Eisenstein remembered Lucky Luciano in real life and not just when he was played by Eduardo Ciannelli.

"Mr. Luciano," Mr. Eisenstein said, "was the spitting image of a gentleman. He wore silk suits and spats and spoke very nicely." Mr. Eisenstein said that all the big gangsters seemed like gentlemen. "If you ran into any of them on the streets," he said, "you would think they were stockbrokers for a living."

Mr. Eisenstein pointed out that in real life and a lot of times in movies, the look of a criminal was deceiving. "Appearances, in that particular line of work, had to be a cover. It wouldn't do to have 'gangster' tattooed on your forehead, would it? Ordinary, respectable looking people really made for the best cons. Remember, Audrey, Alec Guinness in *Kind Hearts and Coronets?*" he asked me. "A priest was a great disguise. Who would have ever suspected a priest?"

This was an angle I would have to consider more.

"You know what else about a famous gangster of my youth?"

"No. What?"

136

"Dillinger. You've heard of Dillinger?"

Of course I'd heard of Dillinger. The famous John Dillinger. Who hadn't? The guy was notorious.

"I'll bet you didn't know," Mr. Eisenstein said, "that Dillinger was a big movie fan. They say it was his downfall in the end. That's how they got him. Melvin Purvis and his G-men found this out and ambushed Dillinger right outside the theatre. He had just seen *Manhattan Melodrama* with Clark Gable. That was his last movie. They made a movie about it with Warren Oates as Dillinger. Maybe I'll get it sometime. With the Gable movie it might make a good double feature. Would you like that?"

"Would I ever," I said. That was one of the finest pieces of scoop I'd ever picked up. The way I figured it, this information put me practically in the same ballpark as John Dillinger.

I was tempted to let Mr. Eisenstein in on the fact that someday there'd be a movie based on my life too, right up there on his silver screen. He could tell all the kids who came to see my movie, "She was a first-rate movie fan. Second only to John Dillinger. She came here every day when she wasn't pulling jobs." Most likely he'd have my seat bronzed the way Gertie did with my baby shoes.

The only problem with my telling Mr. Eisenstein about how someday there was going to be a movie based on my life would be my having to add what that movie was going to be about. Even though Mr. Eisenstein was aces in my book, and I knew for certain he wouldn't squeal to the coppers, he was still a grown-up. Grown-ups are under contract to set you straight.

Also, if I told him about my illegal activities, that would make Mr. Eisenstein an accomplice, which meant he could have gone to the slammer on my account. This would be almost certain to happen because Mr. Eisenstein wouldn't turn me in. He'd keep his lip buttoned no matter how the law tried to pry information out of him. That's the kind of hairpin he was.

My secret had to remain a secret for now. Once I got famous and my mug was plastered all over the front pages, then Mr. Eisenstein would know. Until that happened, it was best to keep mum and talk some more about other people's dark doings.

"So what makes a Western a bad Western instead of a good Western?" Mr. Eisenstein asked me.

"Huh?" Off in the land of my own movie, I hadn't been listening. I'd thought we'd been talking about gangsters.

"A bad Western," Mr. Eisenstein said, "is when they put the bad guys in black hats and black shirts and put them riding black horses. They might as well carry signs, no? The point is, Audrey, the bad guy shouldn't look so much like a bad guy."

I took Mr. Eisenstein's word on this. After all, he'd seen about ten thousand and two more movies than I had. He had to know what he was talking about. "The idea is to be above suspicion," he said.

Once I thought about that, wasn't that how I pulled off such a clean job with the mosaic box? I didn't look anything like the picture of a gangster. No one would suspect a shrimpy kid of making off with big-time loot. My best cover was to be myself. It was the first time ever that being too short and undeveloped was okay by me. It felt good. Real good.

It was excellent timing having this talk with Mr. Eisenstein when I did. I'd had this plan about changing my image to fit the picture of the newest hood to hit Brooklyn. My intentions were to ditch those plaid jumpers Gertie favored and to wear floozy clothes instead. I was going to steal myself a whole new wardrobe. Including new shoes.

To get the shoes, I was going to employ an old, old con. I'd planned to try on every single pair in the store until there were only two pair left; a pair of red high heels and royal blue cowboy boots. While I had the red high heels on, I'd send the salesman for the boots. "Size four narrow," I'd remind him, knowing all the while that cowboy boots didn't come in that size. I knew this from previously wanting a pair desperately. When the salesman went on his quest, I'd bolt as fast as I could on red high heels—out of Shoes, past Hosiery, beyond Gloves and out the door. It was an old con but those are the best cons. Tried and true and all that.

This stroke of luck and common sense altered those plans. I had to wonder why I'd ever considered changing my looks when they were a natural disguise. With my size and shape and angelic mug, I could have cleaned out Latson's on one afternoon. I was a goldmine of deception.

"You want another soda, Audrey?" Mr. Eisenstein

asked after listening to me suck at the ice chips through my straw. "On me," he offered. "My treat."

"No can do, Mr. Eisenstein. Thanks anyway. I've got an appointment," I said.

THE LIFE was within reach. I figured I was almost a professional. Even though I remained careful, clipping two-bit merchandise only, I knew in my guts it was but a short time before I'd be making off with very fenceable items. Boosting stuff like stereo equipment and diamonds was in the stars for me.

In one week alone, I lifted a lipstick called Honeysuckle Red, a pair of ultrasheer pantyhose, a compass (the kind you draw circles with), a baby's rattle, a cream that was supposed to reduce puffiness under the eyes, and a bottle of lavender-water perfume. On Friday, in one brief spree, I was good for a pair of men's socks (gray), blue nail polish with silver sparkles in it, a hairband, and a change purse shaped like a fish. Quite a haul, I'd say, especially since I'd had to take Thursday off for Thanksgiving.

Of all that loot, the pantyhose were the heist I was the most proud of. Not because they were the most valuable (I think the eye cream had the steepest price tag) but because they required a different technique. All the other junk fit neatly into the palm of my hand for the disappearing act. That type of job had become a breeze, as easy as breathing. There was nothing to getting an item in my pocket or, with a well-placed scratch, down my pants. Little girls scratch themselves all the time. No one looks twice at that, and mean-while, I've got nail polish nestled in my underwear.

The pantyhose, packaged flat in cardboard, fit in neither resting place. Using my wits, I developed a new method right on the spot.

My schoolbooks were my accomplice, providing the necessary diversion. I happened to be carrying an arm-load and a half of books with me, due to some chemical in the air which caused all the teachers at school to be monsters on the same day. They piled on the home-work the way Wimpy stacked up hamburgers in Popeye cartoons.

As I never went to the store with a particular item in mind, I had no thoughts about stealing something so oddly packaged until my books slipped. It was then that the idea of stealing pantyhose came to me in a vision.

The second time my books slipped it was on purpose. I let them fall all the way to the floor. With a sheepish grin on my puss as if to say, "Silly me. Clumsy me," I scooped them up. A pair of ultrasheer pantyhose just happened to slip between my science book and a blue binder. By mistake, I took the package home.

My loot barely fit in my drawer. Each night, after my day's work, I would take everything out and spread it on the floor before me. Examining each item one at a time, I'd replay in my head the details of the job, what risks had been involved and how I'd outsmarted them all.

This was not unusual behavior. In the movies, very

often the gangsters would take their loot from the hiding spot and run their hands through it. Usually, their loot was cash or gems but the same principles were at work here. Gangsters fondle their haul just for the kick of it.

The next thing I did was to take a nightly tally of how much this stuff was worth in cold, hard dough terms. To date, my haul was valued at almost forty dollars, not including tax. After adding the figures and double-checking my addition, I quoted another top flight gangster—Edward G. Robinson. "I want more," Edward G. and I both said. "Yeah, more. That's what I want. I want more." It takes a real criminal at heart to appreciate a line like that. I got it from *Key Largo*.

ON SATURDAY, I left the house early, taking time only to get dressed and have a bowl of Raisin Bran. The Raisin Bran was Gertie's idea. It was faster to eat it and be done than to argue with her about why I didn't want breakfast.

Taking no detours, I went directly past go to the bus stop and got off at the mall.

It was fate which brought me to Lana's Boutique. As a rule, I'd been avoiding the small shops. Small shops have too many salespeople and not enough customers for me to blend into the woodwork. Small shops are risky.

I was trying to make my way through the walkway to the department stores but the holidays were coming and half of Brooklyn was at the mall. I was having a hard time pushing past the shoppers when an announcement came over the loudspeaker: "Lana's Boutique is offering the sale of the century. Two for the price of one on everything." This announcement brought a tidal wave to Lana's. I got swept in with it and found myself surrounded by fat ladies behind the jewelry counter. I couldn't see over or beyond them. Letting my reflexes take over, my hand shot up like a periscope on a submarine rising out of a sea of fleshy waistlines.

Groping until my hand touched base, I took the first object I felt and pulled my hand back. Politely covering my mouth, I coughed. Whatever it was in my hand I slipped under my tongue.

I squeezed my way out, ducking under legs and crawling between hips and thighs and stomachs. I was half hoping some flatfoot would tell me to empty my pockets while I had the goods in my mouth. But no one did and I made it downstairs to the restrooms. I locked myself in a stall after peeking under the other ones to make sure the law wasn't lurking about. Then I spit whatever it was in my mouth into my hungry hands.

My good fortune was amazing. Even blinded by all the ladies, I had managed to grab what had to be the classiest item in Lana's Boutique. Maybe even the classiest in the entire mall. This was a rare pinch. I'd snatched an unbearably pretty diamond and pearl ring set in gold.

This ring looked familiar to me. I was certain I'd seen it somewhere before. Then it came me. I had seen one like it on Jean Harlow's finger. In the movie *Reckless* she wore a ring which looked just like this one. I remembered the way the camera caught the sparkle each time she waved her hand about.

I rounded out the day by lifting and pocketing a spoon from Housewares at Latson's, a package of tissue (the purse-sized pack) from the drugstore department, and a Chapstick from the same counter.

Returning to the bathroom, I took out my stolen tissues and opened the cellophane wrapping. Then I flushed all the tissues down the toilet but one. With the last tissue I blew my nose and threw the used tissue in the trash bin along with the Chapstick. I'd already clipped tissues and Chapstick on a prior job and didn't want doubles in my loot. There wasn't room left in my drawer for doubles. Nor for stuff I didn't really need. I was throwing away a lot of the stuff I'd stolen.

The loot I saved was things like the sparkle nail polish and the nail file which might someday come in handy. I also kept the loot that had sentimental value. And I kept the *Frank Sinatra Sings Christmas Songs* album because that job represented a step up. It was practically on the very professional level due to the goods' size and shape. That Frank Sinatra record was almost something I could've brought to the crime bosses to prove my worth.

Declaring my day a lucrative one and not wishing to press luck any further, I left the mall. When I got outside I looked up at the digital clock in front of the bank. It was already after four, which meant it was too late to go to the movies.

I felt bad about that. All week long I'd missed my movies because there weren't enough hours in the day to go to the movies and work out the script for the movie based on my life.

That afternoon, Mr. Eisenstein was showing *The Birds*, a four-star Hitchcock classic. I'd seen it before but on television. Mr. Eisenstein said to watch a movie like *The Birds* on television was to slaughter it.

I'd been really looking forward to seeing it on the big screen. The others I'd missed that week were *Dead End*, the 1937 remake of *Madame X*, and *The Inspector General*. In other words, I'd missed out in a big way.

The way I figured it, going to school was interfering with my life—only I couldn't figure a way out of it. I'd have to learn to commit my crimes on a more rapid basis.

WHILE IT was my usual practice to keep all stolen items well hidden from my mother's sharp eye, I decided to break that tradition and wear the Jean Harlow ring. I couldn't bear the thought of keeping it in my desk drawer. Luckily it had an adjustable band. I squeezed the band tighter and tighter until it fit my index finger. I don't think I could have made it go any smaller without the gold snapping in half.

Gertie must have been losing her stuff. It took her until Monday morning to spot the ring on my finger. Over breakfast, with just her and me at the table, she made eye contact with the hot ice. She reached across my plate of scrambled eggs and clamped her hand on mine. "What is this?" she asked.

"A ring," I said. "What does it look like?"

Gertie told me not to get smart with her. "I know perfectly well what it is. What I want to know is where you got it."

I was very well aware at that moment that wearing the ring was not one of my smarter moves. But I was so excited about wearing it to school, I didn't think too clearly. The dolls at my school were big jewelry hounds. My ring was bound to cause a stir. Those girls in my classes were always yapping about real gold this and real gold that. Some of them had real gold lockets. With diamond chips in them. Those diamonds were specks of dust compared to the rock I had on.

On a couple of occasions I had asked Gertie if I could have a real gold locket but she told me I was too young for real gold. At times like that, Gertie often forgot how old I was. Even though she was there on the day I was born.

"It's a friendship ring," I said. As it had been a while since I'd fibbed about having friends when I didn't, I figured it was a fresh enough lie to be believed. To make it on the streets, it is necessary to be as skilled at lying as at pocketing the goods. Lying and stealing go together the way peanut butter and jelly do. "Lying thief" is practically one word. "It was given to me by my best friend at school," I said. "It's real glass," I said. I would have bet it all that Gertie had no idea "glass" was what gangsters called diamonds.

"Still, it's very pretty," she said. If they did the movie of my life, this scene would have been a close-up of Gertie buying my story. We would have seen her face soften. If Gertie were played by a first-rate actress, and not some ham, we would have seen a wisp of guilt in her eyes—over the fact that she didn't trust me one hundred percent. Then the camera would have switched angles. It would have zoomed in on me as I told the rest of my story. "All the girls at school were giving each other friendship rings. You know, you give it to the one you want to be your best friend. It's like going steady but different. Velda McDonald gave me this one." Velda was the name of Mike Hammer's secretary from Mickey Spillane.

Gertie ate that slop right up. All mothers of gangsters believe their kids' stories right up until the very end. They insist their kid is a good kid no matter how long his rap sheet is. In many circumstances, mothers were made to be lied to.

If it weren't for the fact that this lie was covering up my illegal activities, it would have been a twinkie lie. It's twinkie behavior to pretend you have a best friend when you don't. Cynthia Herman, this girl at school who was a regular at the loser's lunch table because she had green teeth and skin to match, used to make up lies about a boyfriend she claimed to have. She said he lived in Queens which is why no one ever saw him. I said he lived in her head. Cynthia Herman spent her weekends picking at her face and not brushing her teeth and no more had a boyfriend than I did. I, at least, had the dignity and brains not to make one up. One Monday morning Cynthia Herman showed up to school sporting an I.D. bracelet with "Jason" engraved on it which we all knew she had bought for herself. It was very pathetic. I wanted to pull her aside and say, "Cynthia Herman, don't you realize no one buys the bit about the boyfriend in Queens? Don't do this to yourself." I didn't do it because I didn't want Cynthia Herman getting any ideas that I liked her.

My lie really wasn't at all like Cynthia Herman's. Mine was just a cover.

"So," Gertie wanted to know, "how is it I never met your friend Velda? Are you ashamed of your home? You shouldn't be ashamed of your home, Audrey. You have a very nice home and a family that loves you. I know most girls your age feel ashamed of their parents. It's a phase you go through. Remember, I was once your age."

Gertie said that a lot, that business about her once having been my age. Of course, I knew this was true. No one shows up on the earth fully grown. However, if anyone could have done that, I suspect my mother would have been the one. I just couldn't get a handle on the picture of Gertie as a kid. I never believed Gertie was really the cut-up she claimed to have been.

"We're not so bad," she went on, "that you can't bring your friend home for cookies and milk."

"Gertie," I asked, "do you think Baby Face Nelson's mother made him cookies and milk after a hard day of pulling bank jobs?"

"Don't call me Gertie. I'm your mother. Show some respect and what does Baby Whossis have to do with your friend?"

"Nothing. I was just wondering."

"So," Gertie said, "it's settled. You'll bring your little friend over today."

"No can do, Gertie." Once you get started in the

business of lying, there really isn't any stopping it. "Velda has to go straight home from school every day. She doesn't have a father," I said. "Her mother has to work long hours ironing shirts in a laundry to support them. She's a sad woman, the mother. Tired all the time. You know who she looks like?"

Although Gertie was not a movie fan by any standards, she was fond of comparing the looks of people we knew to movie stars. According to her, my brother Alex looked like Richard Gere and Mr. Ellis who lived on the first floor was a Johnny Carson double. Gertie said I looked exactly like a young Natalie Wood!

"Velda's mother," I said, "is the spitting image of Majorie Main. She always looks beat as if the world's got the better of her. She wears her hair in a ratty bun. A sad woman, Gertie. A sad woman who dresses in faded cottons and flat shoes because her feet hurt from standing all day in the laundry."

Gertie wanted to know what happened to Velda's father so I told her. "Drank," I said. "And ran off with some chippie."

This was the brand of soap opera Gertie adored. She loved having her heart wrenched, so I tugged on the strings some more. "Velda has a little sister who is paralyzed," I said. "The way Velda tells it, the kid was lucky she wasn't killed. Crushed by a hit-and-run bus. Velda says when she gets some money she's going to hire a gumshoe to track down her old man and the creep who ran over her sister."

"A gumshoe?" Gertie could be ignorant when she wanted to.

"A gumshoe. A P.I. A detective. Like Philip Marlowe."

"Oh," said Gertie. "And are there other children?"

"There were." I hung my head to indicate further tragedy.

Gertie was sick with grief for my friend Velda. "So much heartache in one family. It hardly seems real."

"Yeah," I said. "So you see why she can't come over after school. She has to take care of things. The paralyzed sister can't even go to the bathroom without Velda."

My mother was wiping a tear from her eye when I slid my chair from the table and got up. "I have to go now," I said. I was tired of this tear-jerker saga, only Gertie was not about to let the curtain close so easily. She made another tuna fish sandwich for me to take to school for my friend. "Audrey—" Gertie whipped the mayonnaise into the red bowl—"I know that the girl gave you that ring out of friendship but they are poor people, no?"

It's amazing how much tragedy Gertie could handle first thing in the morning. "Dreadfully poor."

"So maybe you should give the ring back to her. Maybe it's all she's got in the world."

"Maybe," I said, "but it might hurt her feelings. She has a lot of pride. She wouldn't like it if I thought of her as poor." The nicest part about making up a friend is I could give her any qualities I chose. Add a line or two, rewrite a scene and presto—I've got the perfect best friend.

Gertie put the second sandwich in my bag. "Wait,"

151

she said. She fumbled with her purse and fished out two dollars. "Here. Take your friend out for an ice cream after school today."

"Hey, thanks," I said. "That's square of you, Gertie. This will mean a lot to Velda."

For one minute there, I almost believed that too.

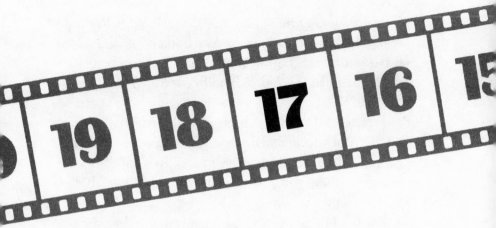

SALLY BELOIT was the sort of dame who could sniff out gold from two hundred yards off. I should have known she'd be the first one to spot my bejeweled finger. Even though she was sitting behind me in homeroom, I could feel her eyes fastened to my hand.

With the eraser part of her pencil, Sally poked me in the back, which was a snotty way to get my attention. But what did I expect? Sally Beloit was a snotty girl and enormously popular. The way I figured it, those two things went hand in hand. What I didn't know was which came first.

"Is that real?" she asked when I turned myself, and my hand with the ring on it, to see why Sally had poked me. As if I didn't already know.

"Is what real?" I asked.

"Your ring," Sally said. "Is it real?"

"Of course it's real," I said. Just to prove it, I made

153

up a convincing lie which made it real and better than real. "It used to belong to Ma Barker," I said. This was even better than it being Jean Harlow's ring.

"Who's that?" Sally Beloit asked. "Your grandmother?"

I started filling Sally in on just who Ma Barker was. "A corrupt mother like none of us has ever known," I said. "She turned her boys into outlaws and was the leader of their gang. In the movies, she was Shelley Winters and . . ."

"And who cares . . ." Sally only wanted to see the ring. "Let me look at it," she said.

I slipped the ring off my finger and dropped it into Sally's outstretched palm. She studied it, turning it inside out, like a pawnbroker. I thought for sure Sally was going to pull out a jeweler's glass, the sort that screws into your eye.

"Fake," she pronounced. "Your grandmother doesn't know real diamonds from rhinestones. Still," Sally Beloit slipped my ring on her pinky, "it is sort of pretty. For a piece of junk, that is."

When she tried to give the ring back to me, Sally Beloit discovered her fingers were fat. The ring stuck fast and wouldn't come off. Although it was a snap to make the ring smaller, it apparently was not the same breeze to make it bigger. Sally gritted her teeth and yanked but the ring did not budge. "It won't come off," she said.

"Forget it," I said. "You can have it."

"It better not turn my finger green," she warned me.

Then Sally positioned her hand just so, admiring her newest jewel. She dipped and flipped her hand around the way my sister Ruth's friend Joyce did when she got engaged. Joyce couldn't bear for anyone not to notice her engagement ring so she flipped her hand around like it was a fish out of water.

During algebra, while Mr. Brandon was explaining some nonsense about x's and n's, I got to thinking about how the ring did take on the story I'd given it. That it had become a friendship ring. There didn't seem to be any way Sally Beloit could not be my friend under these circumstances. Maybe not best friends but enough of a friend that I wouldn't have to eat lunch by myself anymore. And after we had lunch together a bunch of times, there'd be no telling how close we'd become.

I'd be Sally Beloit's friend of a lifetime. The way I figured it, Sally must have had a list several miles long of trinkets she had to have, and would perish without, and I could steal them for her. She would want eyeshadow and French barrettes and doo-dads that don't do anything. And I would swipe them for her.

Even though she hadn't shown much interest in Shelley Winters as Ma Barker, I had the feeling that, deep inside, Sally Beloit had the makings of a real movie fan. All she needed was someone like me to steer her away from the duds and lead her to the greats. Mr. Eisenstein would be very impressed with her. "Another Carole Lombard," he'd call her.

I hurried to the cafeteria with the idea of strolling

by Sally's lunch table where she'd catch my eye. "Audrey," she'd say, "why don't you join us for lunch?" To which I planned on replying, "Well, I'm supposed to lunch with someone else but I guess I can sit for a couple of minutes."

It appeared I was a bit anxious. When I got there, Sally's lunch table was empty. I'd forgotten that Sally and her crowd spent half the lunch hour in the bathroom fixing their makeup. I had to stroll by their table a good fifty-seven times before Sally and company showed up.

The way I figured it, my plan would have worked just fine if that Jennifer Sheldon wasn't around. Jennifer Sheldon had golden-blond hair. Around Canarsie, that made her something of a Marilyn Monroe. I would have bet anything that blond hair came straight out of a bottle, a peroxide blond if ever there was one. "You looking for something?" Jennifer Sheldon said to me.

They all snickered at that. Even Sally Beloit laughed. Sally Beloit seemed to have clear forgotten I'd given her, and she'd accepted, a ring that was practically a friendship ring, only a few hours earlier.

In the movie world, Sally Beloit would get hers. Back at my own private, personal lunch table, I saw the movie of this in my head as vivid as if I were sitting at the Variety and we were on the screen. Some years from now, according to this script, I'd have bosoms and be a glamorous doll. I'd be on my way home from having painted the town red with my friends. These

156

friends were underworld figures and movie stars who kept me in fur stoles and real diamonds. No cheap pieces of glass for me. My girlfriends would be famous torch singers. Sally would be standing on a street corner under the glow of a streetlight. She would be still waiting for her geeky date who had pulled a no-show. Who could blame him? Sally Beloit would be looking cheap and haggard. I'd strut by, confident on my spiked heels and say, "Hey, Sally Beloit. How's tricks?" And I'd keep on walking and I wouldn't even wait to hear how she was.

Anyway, friendship rings are for twinkies. I never took that stuff seriously. I wouldn't even trade friendship rings with Rosalie when she wanted to, and we were little kids then.

THAT AFTERNOON, I made off with a screwdriver from the hardware store in the mall. It was a deliberate hit in the sense that I knew what I wanted when I went in. I intended to learn how to jimmy locks. From the movies I'd gathered that a screwdriver was the best tool for that trade. The heist itself was a simple one although it took some time for the opportunity to present itself. There was only one man working in that store but it wasn't a big place. From behind the counter, he had an eagle's eye view of the whole shop. I had to hang around and wait until another customer wanted something from the storeroom. It seemed forever before that happened but finally some lady came in with a list of screws she needed. She handed the man the list and he said, "I'll be back in a minute." That minute was all it took. I dropped the screwdriver into my pocketbook and was out of there.

Unfortunately, the delay of waiting around to make my move caused me to miss my movie. So, I went straight home. I sat around the kitchen and flipped through *TV Guide*.

Due to sports events and holiday specials, which were sub-twinkie viewing material, there was no Eight O'clock Movie scheduled. This was a terrible disappointment. But all was not lost. At eleven-thirty, *It's a Wonderful Life* was on. And not only that. It was on the educational channel which meant there wouldn't be any dopey commercial interruptions. After that discovery, the lack of an eight o'clock movie did not seem anywhere near as grim. With *It's a Wonderful Life* to look forward to, I was able to make it through the evening.

At eleven-twenty-five, when everyone was asleep, I crept out of bed and opened the bedroom door. The apartment was dark. I started my tiptoed trek to the living room, lifting each foot high and bringing it down slow which was another trick I'd learned at the movies. That's how cat burglers walk. So do men and women sneaking in and out of bedrooms where they don't belong. You don't make a peep when you walk like that.

As I made my way around the corner, I was extra careful because that was the danger zone. Around that bend was my parents' room. I was about to bring my left foot down when I caught sight of a strip of light at

158

the bottom of the door. This wasn't a regular thing. Usually, their light is out by ten. I paused and then stepped in closer to make what I could of this. Were they awake? Or had they fallen asleep with the lights on? Not daring to so much as breathe, I held my breath. Gertie had super-sonic hearing and would often detect a person in the next building coughing.

I pinned my ear to their door to listen for Herb's snoring. Herb was good for a whopping snore which sounded like a jet plane landing every thirty seconds or so. I was listening for the blast.

What I heard instead was Gertie. She was talking in that stage whisper of hers. "It's getting serious," she said. "I tell you. It's worse."

As Gertie tended to make very big deals out of air bubbles and could have been talking about nothing more than dish towels and how often they wear out, I was about to move on. I wasn't going to miss the opening of *It's a Wonderful Life* to eavesdrop on one of her tales of woe.

I would have gone directly to the waiting TV set if I hadn't caught Herb's response. "She's a little girl. All little girls make up stories."

I had this feeling in my gut that I didn't want to hang around and listen to this but I could not move. My feet ignored my command to walk and refused to budge.

"She's not a little girl anymore, Herb," I heard Gertie say. "We forget that. She's a teenager. And teenagers don't make up such stories."

I tried to figure out which lie it was that Gertie had

159

caught on to. The trouble was there were so many of them, I couldn't even take a guess.

"You should have heard today," Gertie said. "It nearly broke my heart. She made up a friend again. She said the friend gave her this ring she was wearing. Some piece of junk she must have bought with her allowance. But she says this friend gave it to her. Then she gives the friend a name and a whole family history. Velma, she called the girl."

It was Velda, I wanted to shout. Not Velma. Velda. Like from Mickey Spillane. Gertie never got anything straight.

"She made it all up because she wanted me to believe she had someone. The phone never rings for her. She spends every afternoon at the movies by herself."

"I thought you told her no movies on school days," Herb said.

"I did. But what am I going to do? Make her stay at home by herself? At least she's out of the house. I was hoping she'd made a friend there. I'm telling you, Herb, I feel so sorry for that kid I could just cry."

Feel sorry for me? Feel sorry for me? My head was screaming with things I wanted to say. Gertie had no reason to feel sorry for me. Not when I was well on my way to becoming a famous gangster right up there with the big ones. Didn't I, just that very day, clip a screwdriver because I was ready to move up the ladder? They're going to make a movie based on my life and Gertie was feeling sorry for me? They'd never make a movie based on her life. How dared she feel sorry for

160

me? "Do you hear me?" I yelled before I could stop myself.

"Audrey?" Gertie called out. "Oh Herb, it was Audrey. She heard us."

"Us?" asked Herb. "I didn't say anything."

I hightailed it back to my bedroom and dove into bed. I was doing a fair acting job of being asleep by the time Gertie showed up. She sat on the edge of my bed. "Audrey," she asked, "are you awake?"

"No," I said. "Go away."

"Can we have a little talk?"

"No. I'm sleeping. Hit the road." I put the pillow over my face.

The very worst part about that scene was I missed *It's a Wonderful Life*. I vowed never to forgive Gertie for that. She had to go and open her mouth like a stoolie and make me miss a Jimmy Stewart movie. A classic. I was going to hold that against my mother forever. Or for a very long time. I'd show her.

20 19 18 17

I WOKE UP to the sounds of Gertie calling my name. She was standing over my bed. Rather than have to look at her, I turned away toward my nightstand and saw, from my clock, that it was way past the time I should have gotten up. Actually, I should have been in algebra instead of in bed.

"I let you sleep late," Gertie said. "I didn't have the heart to wake you. I made pancakes. Your favorites. You'd like some nice pancakes and maybe we'll spend the day together? You can have a little holiday."

If Gertie thought she could babble her way out of the night before, she was sorely mistaken. I pulled the covers over my head until she went away.

Weekday mornings provided some good television on reruns. I decided not to let them go to waste, and set myself in front of the TV just in time for *Leave It to Beaver*. Twice during the show, Gertie came in with the offer of pancakes still good. No matter how hungry

162

I was or how much I liked pancakes, I wasn't going to give in. I wouldn't break. I would never eat food prepared by Gertie's hands again.

After *Beaver* I watched *The Odd Couple* and *Bewitched*. Then, there was a movie on called *Kentucky* which starred Loretta Young and Walter Brennan. It was about family feuds. I guess it was an okay movie although I found it hard to concentrate on. My mind was caught up with other things. Mostly on how I wasn't going to be able to stay in this house much longer. Not with Gertie doubting my every word. I was definitely going to have to take another step up the ladder to criminal success. I was going to have to start clipping items of real cash value. Stuff like stereo equipment and fur coats and real diamonds and emeralds. I was going to have to graduate from this nickel and dime kids' stuff.

Toward the end of the movie, Gertie came into the living room carrying a tray which she set down beside me. "You must be famished," she said. "I made you a little something to eat."

On the tray was a chicken sandwich on whole wheat, a glass of milk and a pink Hostess Sno-Ball. Gertie knew I was wild about Hostess Sno-Balls. But I resolved to be strong. "Go away," I said.

"Please eat something." Gertie believed that all the world's troubles could be solved with food.

In no uncertain terms, I told her I was not hungry.

"Maybe later," Gertie sniffled. "Maybe later you'll be hungry." She left the tray where it was.

In prison, hunger strikes are daily routine. Cons are

163

always going on hunger strikes. There wasn't any reason I couldn't have gone on one, too. Except that I was starving and that Hostess Sno-Ball, that pink marshmallow-covered chocolate cake decorated with shredded coconut proved to be irresistible.

I swore to myself I'd only eat the coconut, picking it off so neatly it would look as if it hadn't been touched. Only I couldn't help myself and, in the end, I polished off the entire Sno-Ball. Maybe Gertie wouldn't notice. Maybe she wouldn't remember there was a Sno-Ball there to begin with. I licked my finger and picked up the crumbs, the shreds of evidence, and made them disappear.

After a little thought on that subject, I realized I was kidding myself. Gertie wouldn't forget about the Sno-Ball. It was put there as temptation so I figured what was done was done. There was no reason now not to drink the milk and eat the sandwich too. I'd start my hunger strike later when I wasn't so starving.

When the movie ended, I consulted *TV Guide* and saw there was nothing else on of interest. Just game shows and soap operas. It was time for me to get moving. I had business to attend to. A job to pull.

I went to my room to get dressed. I took off my pajamas and decided they weren't dirty—I could get one more night out of them. Mostly, I decided this because it made Gertie crazy when I put used clothes back in the drawer. "It's too much effort to use the hamper?" she'd ask.

I folded the pajamas up in a ball and opened the

drawer. There, on top of my regular pajamas, was the Heather Locklear Sleepwear Gertie had bought for me. It was still in the cellophane since my last birthday. Heather Locklear pajamas were strictly feeb wear. "But Heather Locklear is a big star," Gertie had said. I had gotten annoyed at Gertie for buying them but afterward felt kind of sorry about that. It wasn't Gertie's fault they didn't make flannel pajamas with Lana Turner's picture on them. Still, I didn't feel so sorry about it that I'd wear them. For some crazy reason, the sight of those feeb pajamas wrapped in cellophane at that moment seemed like a scene in a movie, as if the camera had moved in for a close-up—and that made me feel like crying. I slammed the drawer shut.

A CRIMINAL has got to watch at every turn for the slip-up. One mistake can crumble the whole cookie. Sometimes the hit-man drops a monogrammed handkerchief at the scene of the crime. His mistake. Some gangsters make the fatal error of blabbing to the wrong dame, the sort of dame with a big mouth and an ax to grind. Sometimes, they just have a bad day and should have stayed at home. If you have other things on your mind, your work can be sloppy.

One of the more interesting slip-ups occurred in a movie called *The Asphalt Jungle*. In that movie, Sam Jaffe starred as the greatest criminal mind the world ever knew. He was the genius of the underworld who nearly pulled the perfect caper. But Sam Jaffe slipped up. He slipped up because of a girl and a juke box.

What happened was that the caper had been pulled. He was in the clear and on his way across state lines into freedom when he stopped at a roadside dive. At this dive was the teenage girl. Not a teenage girl like me. This girl was built very well and she liked to dance to the music from the juke box. Sam Jaffe was really liking her dancing so he gave her a handful of change and sat back to watch her strut. Sam was getting hot under the collar. He knew the law was on his tail and he had to get going. But Sam Jaffe couldn't take his eyes off the girl. He kept handing her more change. The girl dropped one more nickel in the slot just as the police converged on the roadside dive. Sam Jaffe was surrounded. Sam Jaffe slipped up.

What I really wanted to steal was a VCR so I could watch movies at home. Several times I had approached Gertie and Herb about buying one of those. The way I saw it, the VCR was the greatest invention since the movie camera itself. Only my parents said, "Absolutely not. There is already entirely too much television watched in this house."

No matter what they said, this VCR was an item I needed. First of all, it would keep me from being at the mercy of the TV programmers who don't know the first thing about good movies and what time good movies ought to go on. Also, with a VCR I wouldn't need to take money from Gertie to go to the Variety. It's a sticky situation to take money from a person you are not on speaking terms with. I wondered if Mr. Eisenstein would let me in to the movies on I.O.U.'s. The way I figured it, he might. My word was good. Still, with the VCR, I wouldn't have to worry about that, and I could pocket all the movie tapes I needed. Gertie could keep her two-bit chintzy handouts to herself.

Also, a VCR would be fencable goods. That was the sort of item I could take to the pawnbroker and get cold, hard cash for in return. Making off with such an item about my person would put me in the major leagues.

The only hitch was that I simply wasn't up to such a crime. I knew this the same way I knew I wasn't up to a bank job or a Brinks truck heist. There is a scale and you have to take one step at a time. The pathetic truth was I was still a penny-ante crook. All I had to show for myself was bobby pins and pencils and the like. No real hood would take me seriously with that even if I did have piles of the stuff. But you can't go from magic markers to VCRs in a day. There has to be a middle ground first.

The way I figured it, the spot between penny-ante and big time was a radio. If I could get myself a radio, or several radios, in the course of a week, I'd have that VCR before the new year. Also, I did not own a radio. We had a family one in the kitchen but not something I could carry around with me. It was high time I started taking care of Audrey.

The conditions for this caper were ideal. With only a handful of shopping days left until the holidays, the mall was filled to capacity with people climbing over each other's heads to get at the goods. I got easily lost in the crowd.

The radios were displayed on a shelf behind the

televisions. I paused over some of the deluxe models, the ones with clocks attached and alarms and dancing ballerinas on top. One of the first rules of the underworld is to know your own limitations and to be reasonable. Some jobs have to be turned down because the odds are against you. One of the deluxe radios just wasn't possible. There's no way that ballerina would fit in a pocket or down my pants.

The radio of my dreams would have to be the sort which ran on batteries and transistors. Portable, the sort I could carry in one hand or in my pocket (heh heh). I chuckled in a real thug-like manner over that.

There was one radio shaped like Mickey Mouse's head. I wasn't about to clip that one. The speakers were in his ears. The same went for the Donald Duck, only the sound came from his little blue cap. Those radios were for squirts. Also, they were the cheapest models in the joint. The way I had things figured, I may as well go for the gold. This was no time to consider small peanuts. It was time to be thinking big. Real big.

In this case "real big" meant AM/FM with plenty of dials, and earplugs. I wanted all the extra features that would fit on one radio which could fit into a ski-jacket pocket.

I picked up one which was shaped like a Cabbage Patch Doll. It was kind of cute but hardly my speed. I wasn't in the market for cute. My radio was going to be racy. Something slick. They had one on the shelf shaped like a Coney Island hot dog. The station numbers were set in the mustard. I thought maybe I'd come back for that one another time. It would have made for a good second radio to take to the beach. But first things first.

FIRST HAD to be the red radio in the red leather case. As soon as I saw it, I knew that babe had to be mine. It was calling to me. "I was made for you, Audrey," it said.

It was rectangular in shape and the case was genuine leather, cherry-red genuine leather. This time I wasn't making anything up. The tags even said so: Leather: chry rd. The tags also read $39.95. The way I figured it, $39.95 plus tax put me in the honest-to-goodness gangster category. My spine tingled with excitement.

I picked my radio up. It fit neatly into my hand as if it were made to order. I ran my thumb over the serrated "On" button. Static came out. Not the usual awful static we got off Herb's car radio. This static was Class A. It was almost like music.

Scouting the area, I checked to be sure there were no security guards (a.k.a. retired cops) lurking about. As if I didn't have a thing on my mind, I surveyed the floor while whistling an innocent tune. Something from *Top Hat* which Fred Astaire sang.

A lady bearing a very strong resemblence to Mrs. Finster from 5C in my building looked over at me. This dame was wearing black stretch pants which were at least two sizes too tight. And she had rollers in her hair not even covered with a scarf. She took a minute from her drooling over a microwave oven to smile at me. In return I gave her my best sweet little girl grin. She went back to her business which was flipping over the price tag of her microwave. For my purposes, the coast was clear.

With my radio still in my hand, I reached into my pocket like all I was after was a stick of Juicy Fruit gum. I fiddled around in there until I was certain the radio was snug in its place. It wouldn't do to have the goods spill to the floor while I was making my getaway.

I came up empty handed. Shucks—no gum. To be sure the radio wasn't bulging obviously, I patted the outside of my pocket. I knew my trade.

Past the aisle of vacuum cleaners, I strolled, browsed and generally blended in with the other bored kids waiting for their mothers.

Gertie was always complaining about the vacuum cleaner she had. She said it backfired and coughed out twice as much dirt as it sucked in. I considered getting one for her. It wouldn't have been too difficult to conceal one of the small ones in a shopping bag. Then I remembered that I wasn't going to be speaking to Gertie ever again. "Let her steal her own vacuum cleaner," I thought.

I took the down escalator which let me off at the gloves and scarves section. Ruth would have liked one of those hat and scarf sets on display. As Ruth was the only family member I was on good terms with, or at least the only one I was still speaking to, I thought it would be wise to get her a little gift. I'd come back the next day and pick that up for her.

On the door of the main entrance I read the sign about shoplifters again, especially the part about how they would be prosecuted to the fullest extent of the law. "Catch me first," I scoffed, although I rarely thought of myself as a shoplifter. Shoplifting is for kids and crazy old ladies. Not gangsters. We pull jobs.

My left foot had just hit the pavement when I heard someone call, "Little girl. Wait a minute." I turned. It was the Finster look-alike. I wondered what it was she wanted.

Then she let it be known. She wanted me. "Security," she said as her hand shot out and grabbed me by the wrist. "Empty your pockets."

I tried to twist free from her grip but she was one strong dame. Her hold on my wrist was like a vise. I was stuck.

How sneaky of that store to use undercover flatfoots. In my book, plainclothesmen were the same as cheating. It's not playing by the rules and struck me as really unfair. So unfair that I started to snivel. Not a lot. Just a little snivel.

Wait a minute. What's with this squirt behavior? I took hold of myself, pulled myself together. I wasn't about to let her beat me at my own game. No matter what lengths she took to win, I wasn't going to let them get me. I was too good, I thought. "There's nothing in my pockets. Now let go of me."

With one of her claws holding me as tight as ever,

tighter than any pair of handcuffs ever used by the
F.B.I. even, her free hand reached into my pocket and
pulled out my radio. The price tags dangled. "What
do you call this?"

"A radio," I said.

"Don't get smart-mouthed with me, kid. You're in
enough hot water as it is." Hot water. That's the way
Gertie talked. I wondered if Gertie were capable of
doing such a snitch's job.

"You'll never take me alive," I told her.

Only she did. She yanked me back into the store. I
felt like I was being pulled by the ear. She dragged me
past the gloves and scarves. Ruth's outfit went by me
in a blur. "Hey," I asked, "where are you taking me?"

"Upstairs," she said which sounded worse than the
Big House itself.

I let her have it in the shins. I wasn't sure if I got
that stunt from a Bob Hope/Bing Crosby "Road" movie
or from a Little Rascals episode. But no matter. It
worked like a charm. She let go of me to nurse her
leg and I was off at the starting gate.

I blasted past Jewelry and rounded the corner on
Handbags. From the corner of my eye, I could see that
Finster-The-Sequel was on her feet and closing in on
me. I picked up steam.

She chased me through Perfume. This was some
great action scene. A great chase. As we ran, clips of
other great chase scenes rolled in my mind. I saw
Indians on ponies racing to overtake wagon trains,
Steve McQueen on his motorcycle, and Eli Wallach

in a black sedan peeling down the streets of Chicago on a rainy night.

In Underwear, I turned to get a look at the enemy. She was huffing and red in the face. An old cop who was through. Washed up. She'd had it. She was ready for the stable. She didn't have a chance of catching me. I was just about to reach around and pat myself on the back when I crashed. Head on, I smashed into a mannequin wearing boxer shorts. This put an end to my career.

"Upstairs" turned out to be an office on the third-floor staircase landing. We walked up the whole way, all the while I was thinking that this stairwell was an ideal spot for a rubout. "In here." The snitch took me behind an iron door. It could have been curtains for me.

This office was your standard interrogation room. The walls and floors were painted gray. There weren't any decorations about and the only light source was a naked bulb hanging overhead. If this had been a movie, a good director would have glued a couple of dead flies to that bulb to further the grim effect. There was a metal desk with a man seated behind it and a couple of chairs around. I thought the lady flatfoot would shove me into one of those chairs like they do in the movies but she didn't.

The head chump, the one behind the desk, was seated in a swivel chair which he rolled back in order to get a better look at me. He was wearing a shabby suit and he had a fat stomach. He looked like every cop in every movie.

"I'm Mr. O'Malley," he said. That figured. Not only did he look like a cop but he had the same name they gave half the cops in Hollywood productions.

He motioned for me to sit in what was probably the hot seat but I outsmarted him and took a different chair. He pretended not to notice. He took a sheet of paper from the desk drawer and a pencil from the pencil box. "You are aware," O'Malley said to me, "it is a criminal offense to shoplift?"

The broad who'd collared me stood at the door blocking it in case I tried for another getaway. "Mr. O'Malley is talking to you," she said.

I pointed out to O'Malley that he hadn't read me my rights. "I'm not saying anything until I see my lawyer."

"What did she steal?" O'Malley asked the Finster imposter. Keeping her feet planted by her post, she stretched and slid the radio across his desk. O'Malley examined the radio. After checking out the price tag, which I had the feeling put me in the grand larceny categoy, O'Malley stared cold and hard at me. "Do you have any idea, young lady, what jail is like?"

Did I know what jail was like? Did this joker have any idea how many prison movies were made in the 1930s alone? And that I'd seen at least half of them including *Women's Prison* with Ida Lupino? Of course I knew what jail was like.

O'Malley's pencil was positioned, ready to write. "Name?" he asked me.

I kept mum.

"Name," he repeated.

"I told you already," I said, "I'm not spilling my guts until I see my lawyer."

"You've been watching too much television, kid. I don't have to read you your rights or let you see a lawyer. We're not the police. You don't have any rights here. When we're done with you, we turn you over to the police. Then you'll get your rights read to you."

If O'Malley was trying to scare me, it worked. A little. *Women's Prison* was no picnic of a movie. It featured lady wardens who looked like prizefighters, women with no hearts. It also gave me a peek into life in Solitary.

"I didn't do anything," I said to O'Malley. "It's my word against hers." I cocked my thumb toward the one who looked like Mrs. Finster. The way I figured it, she probably moonlighted as a guard at the local pen.

"We'll try it again, kid," O'Malley said. "What is your name?"

"I'm not talking," I said.

"Age?" he asked.

"Fourteen," I said.

He eyed me up and down. "Don't lie to me. Tell me how old you are."

I told him again. "I really am fourteen," I said. "I'm little because I have a disease. An incurable disease."

"You look pretty healthy to me. Doesn't she look healthy to you, Mildred?"

Mildred. I made a mental note of that stool pigeon's name. I was putting her name on my list. She could have the slot of honor, the place otherwise held by the Bat-Lady.

"She sure acted healthy." Mildred rubbed her shin where I'd kicked her.

"You'd send a sickly kid up the river?" I asked.

"Maybe." O'Malley, the second string G-man, lit up a cigarette. I thought for sure he was going to blow smoke in my face to show his contempt. In the movies, that's a standard piece of interrogation. So is the cop cracking his knuckles to imply that he might use them. Only O'Malley must not have gone to the movies much. He blew his smoke up where it circled and hung around the light bulb. That wasn't a bad touch. It looked like something John Huston would have directed. "Now," O'Malley said, "why don't you quit aggravating me and be a nice kid. Give me your name, age, address, and telephone number."

They could torture me all they wanted. I could take whatever they had to dish out. I drew my inspiration from the tough guys in the movies. I zipped up my lips and threw the key away.

"How long do you want to sit here, kid?" that imitation cop asked. "Because I've got all night. I'm in no hurry. You want to sleep here, it's fine by me." He put both feet up on his desk like that was proving his point.

We both looked at the clock on the wall. It was the sort of clock with a long red second hand designed to tick by real slow. O'Malley took a deck of cards from the top desk drawer and began flipping them over as if to pass the long hours ahead.

I asked him if he was interested in flipping me for my freedom. "High card and I can go," I said, but he acted like he didn't hear what I'd said. Who was this guy trying to kid? He didn't have all night. He wanted to get home to his dinner.

It was 4:48. I got up from my chair and looked out the one small window, so dirty I hadn't even realized it was there. I cleaned it with my arm and saw that we looked out onto a back street. I tried to angle for a break. I wondered if I could scale that window and land on my feet. I'd seen a lot of prison breaks in the movies where that happened but then I remembered the super's mutt. I went back to my chair.

Five-twenty-four. I had to go to the bathroom.

"Tell me your name and Mildred will take you to the bathroom," O'Malley said.

I crossed my legs.

Six-forty-six. Usually I was home by six-thirty at the latest. If I was five minutes later than that, Gertie assumed I'd been kidnapped. At 6:49 Herb would be coming home and Gertie, already having checked the mailbox for ransom notes, would be sending Herb out to look for me by seven.

I felt like I was trapped in a Saturday morning cartoon. I was Daffy Duck on the edge of indecision. On one shoulder sat a little white angel. A tiny red devil perched on the other. Each whispered, in turn, what I should do. My angel looked and sounded a lot like Gertie. "Audrey," she called into my ear, "Audrey. Come home. Please come home. We're all worried about you. Even Alex. Come home."

On the other side, my little devil was a two-inch-tall Robert Mitchum wearing an itsy fedora pulled over one eye. "Don't let them break you, kid," he said. "Bite the bullet."

At six-fifty-nine I apologized to Robert Mitchum, to Cagney and Robinson and Bogart and Al Capone and Jesse James. I said I was sorry to all the tough guys, the cons, the hoods, the gangsters and criminals and outlaws from every movie I'd ever seen. I broke, "I'm only a kid," I said and then I spilled my guts to O'Malley and Mildred. I gave them all the information they were after.

O'Malley wrote it all down and then checked to see if I had a record on file at the store. "First offender," he said. "I'm going to be easy on you," he said, "because it's your first offense. I'm not going to call the police."

Instead, O'Malley dialed my phone number. He was going to rat on me to Gertie and Herb. I fell on the floor and begged him not to do it. Cagney begged once. In *Angels with Dirty Faces*. It didn't get him anywhere either. "My mother has a heart condition," I said. "This could be curtains for her."

"You should have thought of that before you tried to steal a radio," Mildred said. All heart, that one.

In his report to Gertie, O'Malley spared none of the details. They had yakked on the phone for some time when O'Malley held the receiver out to me and asked, "Do you want to speak to your mother?"

I said no thanks.

O'Malley got back on the line and told Gertie he was sending me home now. "She'll be along shortly," he said.

I got up to leave but O'Malley told me to sit down again. "I'm not quite finished with you," he said. "This file," O'Malley waved the paper with my vital statistics on it, "is on a computer file throughout every store in the United States." I had a hunch O'Malley was bluffing but I wasn't in any hurry to test that theory out.

Next O'Malley told me I was banished from Latson's. "You are no longer welcome in this store. Is that understood?"

Not that I'd ever want to shop here again anyhow, but I nodded in recognition.

"Mildred will escort you out. You can go now," he said.

"Aren't you going to fingerprint me and take a mug shot?" I asked. I figured I'd gone this far, I might as well go all the way. Besides, I was kind of interested in getting the booking procedure firsthand.

"I got your mug shot up here," O'Malley tapped at his head. "And I never forget a face."

Mildred led me through the store and out the door like it was the state line. "We're serious," she said, "about your not being allowed in this store again. I don't ever want to see you after this."

"Believe me, Mildred," I said, "I'm none too anxious to look at your face twice either."

I GUESS I should have been filled with remorse about what I'd done. Repentence should have been brimming over. I should have been sorry and eager to change my ways. I tried to think of the bus ride home as the path down the straight and narrow.

The trouble was no matter how hard I tried to convince myself I regretted being a gangster, the best I could muster up was I was sorry I'd gotten snagged. That is the way the criminal mind works. All I was really interested in was getting off the hook.

There was no doubt that Gertie and Herb would be demanding an explanation. This was one of those cases where telling the truth was not the thing to do. The way I figured it, the best explanation would have to be a lie. I needed a lie which would not incriminate me so much. Maybe even one which would clear me altogether.

180

I flipped through the files of movie plots, the file I kept in my head, trying to come up with a story that would lessen my punishment.

The first story I came up with was to blame it on Velda. Velda stole the radio for her invalid sister to have something to keep her company during the long, lonely days. Velda had to steal because she was too poor to afford such a costly item even if she saved for the next ten years. I, in the end, took the rap for her out of the goodness of my heart. Velda's mother wouldn't have survived Velda's prison sentence. I thought that was a first-rate lie. The only hitch was that Gertie wasn't buying Velda's existence in the first place. I could have tried to point out to her that no one believed Jimmy Stewart about Harvey the rabbit's existence either. Only Gertie wasn't so good at connecting the dots and would say something like, "Jimmy Stewart isn't my daughter. I don't care what Jimmy Stewart does."

The second story I came up with was the one I decided to stick with. I'd been framed. According to enough movies, getting framed really happens at least twice a day. It's very common.

"It wasn't me," I planned on insisting. I made up a fairly believable scene, pieces of several movies glued together, about how this man was hovering around me while I was admiring a nice radio which was shaped like Donald Duck. This man was fingering the red radio. This man had a scar running across his forehead. He was dressed in a pin-stripe double-breasted suit and had tattoos on his arms. Before he walked away, he bumped into me and that's when he slipped the radio into my pocket. I didn't think anything of it until I reached in my pocket looking for a stick of gum and found a radio in there instead. I was about to put it back when this lady who looked like Mrs. Finster grabbed me. After they were done roughing me up upstairs, I saw the man outside the store. He was waiting for me. "It's an old trick," I planned on informing them. "If you went to the movies more often, you would know that." The way I figured it, this story would leave me free as a bird.

I had so much confidence in the plot, I wasn't at all worried as I walked the block from the bus stop to our house. Cool as a cucumber, I went upstairs. I opened the door and at the same time, I said, "I was set up. Framed."

I said this before I looked at the dining room table. There, spread out like pastries at a wedding party, was the stuff I'd stolen, my loot: chalk, erasers, Aunt Ida's thimble, the Frank Sinatra album, the nail polish, the eye shadow, the pens. My entire career was laid out before me. Given that kind of evidence, I knew my story wasn't going to hold up.

I looked at my family. They were seated around the goods. Gertie was wiping tears from her eyes. Herb was stone-faced. That "I told you so" grin was plastered across Alex's mug. Ruth was wearing her social-worker look, the one which said, "I can help you," when I knew she couldn't.

182

There was no choice here for me. There was only one thing to do and I did it. I turned and ran. I heard them all calling after me but I didn't stop to answer. I ran down the stairs, out the door, and I understood I was on the lam.

The streets were cold and dark and I was alone in the world. In the movies, this is the moment where the criminal either turns himself in or goes to church. I went to the Variety.

"Audrey!" Mr. Eisenstein seemed surprised to see me. This was understandable because I never went to the movies at night. Also, he hadn't been seeing too much of me these days. "What are you doing here?"

"I came to see the movie," I said. "What's playing?"

"*Meet John Doe*," Mr. Eisenstein said. "Gary Cooper. Barbara Stanwyck. A great movie. A truly great movie. But the next show doesn't start for a half hour. It's okay with your parents you're out so late?"

"No problem," I told him.

"So, good," he said. "Have a seat. I'll go set up the projector. A fresh batch of popcorn will be ready in a minute. We'll have some buttered and a nice talk."

Mr. Eisenstein went into the projection room and I sat back in one of the red velvet chairs. Mr. Eisenstein sure was a straight arrow. He didn't go sticking his nose where it didn't belong. He didn't ask a million questions about what I was doing out so late on a school night or anything. Mr. Eisenstein minded his own business.

I pulled at some loose threads on the chair. This velvet was worn pretty thin. The Variety Theatre was a lot like the chorus-girl gone floozy that you see in the movies. Old and not really pretty anymore but if you look real hard you see there's something special even though she looks beat up.

Someday, I thought, I'd have my own movie theatre. Only I'd keep mine all to myself. My very own private theatre and I wouldn't sell tickets to anyone no matter how much they begged. My theatre would have crystal chandeliers and marble floors and Persian carpets. It would be just like the model of the Roxy and like the movie houses Mr. Eisenstein had told me about. The others from the olden days. "You should have seen the old Rialto, Audrey," he'd said. "It was like the Taj Mahal. And the RKO was as beautiful as Tara from *Gone With the Wind.*" Mr. Eisenstein had told me that everything about going to the movies in those days was a dream. Not just the pictures playing and the selected short subjects. Those were mini-movies shown before the feature. A lot of them had to do with the war effort and were very exciting. Other short subjects were cartoons. The way Mr. Eisenstein told it, the ushers wore snappy uniforms and you got to play bingo at intermissions. They even had live organ accompaniment.

"So—" Mr. Eisenstein stepped behind the popcorn machine and filled up a large bucket—"*Meet John Doe* is ready to roll and we'll be better off in this world when it does." Mr. Eisenstein poured a generous amount of butter on the popcorn and handed it to me. I was very grateful for this. Having missed dinner after an action-packed day, I was starved.

184

Mr. Eisenstein sat down next to me. "Your mother called here looking for you," he said. "Before you got here."

"What did you tell her?" I asked.

"What did I tell her? The truth. No. You weren't here. If I saw you, I told your mother, I would tell you she called. So I'm telling you."

I didn't pay any attention to this information and busied myself with my popcorn.

"She sounded worried," Mr. Eisenstein said, but he had enough good sense to leave it at that. "So," he changed the subject, "you got a boyfriend now?"

That is a question which tended to tick me off. For one thing, adults had this way of asking me that the same way they ask some kid in kindergarten. Real coochie-coo. They expected me to giggle and tug at my underwear and say, "Maybe," so they could have a laugh over how cute I was.

I certainly was old enough to have a boyfriend. My sister Ruth was dating when she was my age, even. Of course, Ruth did have bosoms back then too, although they were still puny. It was also true that I wouldn't have walked around the block with the collection of geeks and drips Ruth dated. But still, she had boyfriends. I wouldn't have minded at all having a boyfriend but I had to keep my feet on the ground about some issues. So, when I was asked, "Do you have a boyfriend?" I found it kind of rude. It was rubbing my face in an obviously bleak situation.

"No," I said to Mr. Eisenstein. "I don't have a boyfriend."

"I only ask," he said, "because I don't see so much of you these days. You want a soda to wash down that popcorn?" He got up to get me one. "Popcorn is nothing without a soda." He gave me a large cherry Coke. Mr. Eisenstein was A-OK.

"I've just been kind of busy," I said by way of explanation about why I wasn't coming around as much as usual.

"It happens," Mr. Eisenstein said. "We grow up and become busy people, and who has time for a movie every day of their lives?"

"I still have time," I said. "I love the movies. I'll always love the movies. I'm a movie fan," I said.

"This is true," Mr. Eisenstein said. "But the movie fan in Audrey is here," he touched his forehead, "and here," he felt his heart. "In between, Audrey, you're going to have a life to live."

I wasn't much liking this talk. I felt like I did when Rosalie told me she was moving to Long Island or when Gertie trashed BaBa, my teddy bear, on the grounds that BaBa was filthy and I was getting too old to be dragging a teddy bear around.

"I think," Mr. Eisenstein said, "Audrey is growing up. I think I won't be seeing so much of my friend Audrey in the future." He held up his hand for me to stop even though I hadn't said anything yet. "This is for the good, Audrey. Movies are like nice dreams but you can't spend your whole life sleeping. You understand me? Movies aren't life."

"Movies are better," I said.

186

"No," said Mr. Eisenstein. "Different. But not better."

Could it have been that Mr. Eisenstein was booting me out? Was he tired of giving me handouts of popcorn and cherry Cokes? Was it that he didn't want to let me in for kid's price any longer and this was his way of breaking it to me?

"Ah Audrey," he said, "you don't think you're the first movie fan to discover taking part in the world instead of watching it on the big screen? You're not the first, Audrey. Not even my good friend Cary Grant can take the place of a flesh-and-blood boy. Viewing the Negev Desert in *Lawrence of Arabia,* as majestic as it can be, can't hold a candle to trudging along the beach at Coney Island. They've come and gone over the years, Audrey. The movie fans. You were one of the best. So maybe it's fitting you should be the last. The end of the line. Maybe," he said, although I had the feeling he wasn't talking to me any longer but to the ghost of Bogart or Clark Gable, "maybe it is time I closed up. Maybe it is time for an old man to put away his movies and go home. Maybe Audrey is the last movie fan. Maybe the silver screen is getting a bit tarnished. Could be."

"Hey, Mr. Eisenstein," I tugged at his sleeve for his attention, which I wasn't sure if I had or not, "what are you talking crazy for? I missed a couple of movies. No big deal."

I really wanted to explain to Mr. Eisenstein why I hadn't been around, that this lapse of mine was tem-

187

porary, that I'd be back to being a movie fan. I wanted to tell him how I was off making the story of my life for the movie they'd make someday. I had to, for those purposes, do other things because if all I did was go to the movies, the movie based on my life would have been boring.

And then I understood that was exactly what Mr. Eisenstein was talking about.

"Go, darling," he said to me. "Go on."

"Go?" I felt like I was about to start bawling. I couldn't believe Mr. Eisenstein was asking me to leave.

"Yes. Go," he said. "Go inside and get a good seat. I want you to get a good seat and not miss the opening credits. They're beauties, those credits. Go."

I got up but before I could actually bring myself to go inside the theatre I said, "Mr. Eisenstein?"

"Yes, Audrey. What is it?"

"You wouldn't close up the Variety on me, would you?"

"No," he smiled. "Not on you, Audrey. Behind you, maybe. But not on you. Now go. Go get a good seat and don't pay so much attention to an old man who spent his life in the dark."

20 19 18

Meet John Doe was a superior movie which made it in a flash to my top-ten all-time favorite list. The plot was sort of complicated but mostly it was about Gary Cooper doing the right thing, being a square shooter in a world which sort of stunk. In this movie, the bad guys were really bad guys, double-crossers and sneaks. It was also an inspiring movie because things didn't look so good for Gary Cooper. He was a ball player with a bum arm but in the end it all turned out aces. I definitely would have sat through this one at least twice but as it turned out, I'd caught the last show. After the other eight people in the theatre cleared out, I hung around and helped Mr. Eisenstein clean up.

"It's a sad place with the lights up, no?" Mr. Eisenstein said to me as we picked up paper cups from the floor. I peeled a Milk Dud off a seat. People are slobs.

189

I asked Mr. Eisenstein if he'd like me to mop or dust. The Variety looked like it could have used a good scrubbing but he said, "No. Thank you but no. It's late. We're tired. It's a big day tomorrow. Tomorrow we've got *Twentieth Century*. John Barrymore. And Carole Lombard's first real comic performance. A gem of a movie."

I left with Mr. Eisenstein. After locking the door he wanted to know if he should walk me home. I said no because I didn't know if I was going home and it didn't seem right to ask him to just walk around with me, what with him being tired.

"You'll be all right?" he asked. "Then I'll be off," and he headed up the block. It was funny. I never thought Mr. Eisenstein lived anywhere except at the Variety.

I walked over to the schoolyard. Not to where I went to school now but to the grammar school. There were swings and monkey bars and seesaws; kid's stuff, but I was sort of in the mood for that. I had had some swell times here back then. Rosalie and I were big seesaw fans. I would have sat on the seesaw now except that one on a seesaw is pathetic. Instead, I went to the parallel bars.

The parallel bars were a constant source of annoyance to me because I was always an inch too short to grab hold. Still, that was where I went. I think that was because I wanted to reach, to stretch for something. I stood underneath and raised my arms, grasping for stars, when my fingers brushed metal.

Slowly, I wrapped my hands around the cold pole and hoisted myself up. I'd grown. I didn't even know it but there I was sitting on the evidence. I'd grown an inch. At least an inch. Maybe two.

I sat up there thinking about other things. Namely, what a twinkie I'd been. Stealing stuff was pretty goofy behavior. Gertie and Herb were bound to be crazed with anger and I couldn't say I blamed them much.

The more I considered it, the more I realized I was sorry. I would wipe the slate clean and start over. In plenty of movies the con goes straight. And after all, I was only fourteen. I deserved a second chance.

If I could just convince Gertie and Herb of that. I tried to think of a way to tell them which didn't sound like a lie but all I could come up with was the truth. All that I could tell them was that I wouldn't do it again. It would have to do. I just hoped they'd buy that.

I dropped down to the ground and walked home.

My block was a ghost town. The streets echoed. But what did I expect? It had to be around midnight. Past bedtime on a school night. Most of the buildings were completely darkened although there were lights on in a few apartments. Mine was one of the lit-up ones.

I stood on the street and looked up at it but couldn't yet bring myself to go inside. So I sat down on the steps. An old tennis ball was lying there on the bottom step. The name Ilene was written on it in black magic marker. It must have belonged to the Jacobson kid in the next building.

Holding the ball in my hands out there on the steps, I could almost see the super's mutt there wagging his tail waiting for me to toss him the ball. I threw it in the air and caught it a couple of times. On the fourth throw, I missed and the ball rolled off under a parked car. Accidents happen.

Like the super's dog. He fell. It was an accident and even though that was sad too, it didn't seem as awful. I wasn't ticked off at the dog anymore because he didn't die on me on purpose.

The door to my building opened. I heard it and turned to see who was there. It was Gertie and Herb. I braced myself for a lot of yelling and was waiting for Gertie to start wailing about how could I have done this to them. Only that didn't happen. Instead, Gertie and Herb joined me on the steps. They sat down. Gertie on one side. Herb on the other.

None of us said a word. We just sat there lined up on the steps all in a row. And I got to thinking that if this were the movie of my life, this picture right here would have made for a swell closing shot.

It would be a nice place to end. A happy ending but not the sort of sappy, happy one where the director whomps you over the head with how happy all the twinkie characters are now that they're reunited. It would have been the sort which makes you use your imagination a little bit. The sort where you know the kid is going to be okay even though you're not told so in as many words.

That's the way I saw it. I saw the camera pulling

back from a close-up until you could see us and the steps and the building. And maybe just a hint of the sky. That's when *The End* would appear on the screen and I would leave the theatre thinking, "Now that's a first-rate end to a movie."

ABOUT THE AUTHOR

Binnie Kirshenbaum lives in New York City and is an instructor of English at Wagner College on Staten Island.

Short Subject is her first novel.